Reunions are *Deadly*

D. M. WYMAN

Best wishes, Linda
D. M Wyman
Nov 2005

NEWEST PRESS

Copyright © D. M. Wyman 2005

All rights reserved. The use of any part of this publication reproduced, transmitted in any form or by any means, electronic, mechanical, recording or otherwise, or stored in a retrieval system, without the prior consent of the publisher is an infringement of the copyright law. In the case of photocopying or other reprographic copying of the material, a licence must be obtained from Access Copyright before proceeding.

Library and Archives Canada Cataloguing in Publication
Wyman, D. M., 1950-
Reunions are deadly / D.M. Wyman.

ISBN 1-896300-98-7

I. Title.

PS8645.Y43R49 2005   C813'.6   C2005-903532-3

Board editor: Lynne Van Luven
Cover and interior design: Ruth Linka
Cover image: J. Alleyne Photography
Author photo: Mylan Photographics

 Canada Council   Conseil des Arts
for the Arts   du Canada

 Canadian   Patrimoine
Heritage   canadien

 edmonton arts council

NeWest Press acknowledges the support of the Canada Council for the Arts and the Alberta Foundation for the Arts, and the Edmonton Arts Council for our publishing program. We also acknowledge the financial support of the Government of Canada through the Book Publishing Industry Development Program (BPIDP) for our publishing activities.

NeWest Press
201–8540–109 Street
Edmonton, Alberta T6G 1E6
(780) 432-9427
www.newestpress.com

1 2 3 4 5 08 07 06 05

PRINTED AND BOUND IN CANADA

To Eldon,
without your support
my dream would have died.

CHAPTER ONE

"What if the storm turns into a blizzard?" Beth McKinney asked as she leaned on the cedar rail of her new veranda.

Mike Ceretzke chuckled as he pulled her against his chest. Her head of curly brown hair barely reached his nose, making her seem petite against his lanky 6'4" body. Beth turned to face him, his fleece jacket rubbing against her high cheekbone and her full lips turning into a smile as he worked the tightness from the muscles of her neck and shoulders.

"You're tense."

"I skipped my run today."

"Worried about blizzards?"

Beth caught the laughter in his blue eyes. "They are forecasting snow. Highways could close, flights could be delayed."

"Don't look for worries. You need snow to cover your perennials and it takes lots of it to cause a blip in the pace of this city."

A chattering echoed through the dim twilight, as a squirrel leapt from a forty-foot spruce onto one of the feeders Beth had strategically placed around her yard. It lifted each peanut until satisfied it held the heaviest, then scampered away. Across the road, two kids struggled to control a beagle intent on exploring the small park. The temperature was in the mid-teens, warm for five o'clock on a November evening, but dropping as the red sunset faded.

Beth moved out of Mike's embrace. "I feel twitchy. It's only a twenty minute walk to the restaurant if we take the riverbank trail."

"Because you missed your 5 KM run?"

"Because I'm going to be shut inside for three days. I need to stock up on fresh air."

"You were the one who fought to hold your class reunion at the Mall," he noted, as she led him toward the trail.

"So their families could have fun too. Besides when there's a local attraction with a worldwide reputation in your backyard, I say use it. Can you think of a better draw than eight hundred stores, a triple loop roller coaster, an ice rink and two mini golf courses?"

"Sure, the Bourbon Street nightclubs that keep the guys on the force busy every weekend," Mike chipped in.

"That's the cynical cop in you talking. Admit you think it's a great place for a reunion."

Throwing his arms wide, he raised his voice and proclaimed, "West Edmonton Mall has everything. It's made the Guinness Book of Records for being the largest shopping mall in the world and for having the largest parking lot."

He paused as an elderly couple approached looking amused. Beth tugged his arm to shush him. Then in a normal voice, he continued, "Half of the poor buggers also get lost in its . . ." he let his voice rise again, ". . . 493,000 square metres, or 48 city blocks, or put yet another way 110 or 115 football fields depending on whether you are talking Canadian or American."

Beth laughed at his spiel. Encouraged, he continued, "Most of the visitors also forget which of the 58 entrances leading to the 20,000 parking spaces will get them to their vehicle."

"And how many of its 23,500 employees work security and are ready to help them find their car?" Beth asked.

"What! You don't know? I thought you knew every fact and figure about the place, unlike me who only needs to know that I'm giving the climbing wall a go and then hitting the Shooting Centre while you stick your cute little nose into every detail of the activities scheduled over the next three days."

"Looking at the neat weapons again?"

"They have some beauties," Mike said.

"You have to keep a few minutes to meet my friends."

"The elusive Trista, unseen for twenty years, and Gina, who keeps a guy in every airport? Believe me I wouldn't miss meeting them for anything."

"Don't forget Jasmine."

"The blushing bride-to-be and her shopaholic daughter. Did they manage to fit all their loot into the car after last month's shopping marathon?"

Beth quickened her pace as her natural walking rhythm took hold. She inhaled the scent of fallen leaves.

"There are so many people I haven't seen since graduation."

"Any old boyfriends you forgot to mention?"

"Did I tell you how many registrants we have?"

"Not more then seven or eight times."

"Okay. I know I'm stuck on that theme."

He reached for her hand. "It's your party and you will make it wonderful."

They strode through the night, wrapped in the mix of traffic noise, animal calls, and rustling leaves until they rounded a turn of the trail and the towers of Edmonton's downtown appeared on the far river bank. Beth paused to admire the lights reflected in the river, then shifted her gaze.

"So many condos. I hate seeing trees cut down so people can take over."

After their Thai dinner, Mike walked Beth home, promising to arrive at the mall as soon as his Friday shift was over. Beth wandered through her house, stopping to play with her cats, black and white Magpie, and Splatter with her multi-hued face.

As usual she gravitated to her office, where she clicked on the computer slide presentation she'd prepared for the reunion banquet. Familiar faces peered at her. Her own grad photo showed a young woman oozing with confidence and ambition. Her expression was free of the worry lines that had appeared so quickly. She'd been open to love back then, before disaster led to her first romantic breakup and the nearly twenty years of broken promises and falling expectations that had followed.

She had kept her figure fairly well, though at one

hundred and thirty pounds she had gained a pound a year. But her cheeks seemed thinner, her cheekbones more prominent, her nose longer.

Her hair was darker now, with a few strands of grey creeping in. Would her friends recognize her?

Other photos flipped onto the screen and she wondered how each person had aged. Part way through she stopped the show. The floppy hair, the cocky smirk. Thank God Wade wouldn't be attending.

It was after two o'clock when she finished reviewing her reunion website and the hundred plus others that featured West Edmonton Mall. After crawling into her queen-sized bed, Splatter crowding her pillow and Magpie warming her feet, she stared at the ceiling. Unable to relax, she reviewed the reunion preparations, imagined every disaster and its potential solutions. Then she dozed, but was drinking coffee on her veranda at eight o'clock when the lazy November sun appeared on the horizon.

CHAPTER TWO

"Beth McKinney! I can't believe you made it this time! Gawd, you look great!"

The woman's squeal pierced the buzz of conversation in the sparsely populated meeting room, causing those gathered around the notice boards to turn, interested in the identity of the voice's owner.

Beth carved twenty years from the woman's sun-wrinkled skin, but the pervasive brown splotches on her massive nose and broad forehead refused to disappear. The padding around her abdomen was soft and her bust was a cushion of flesh.

Beth searched for a dominant colour in the wiry mop of hair. Where was the teenaged girl buried inside this middle aged woman? Only when Beth focused on her nose did she feel a stirring of recollection. The bushy eyebrows provided a final ping to her memory cords. She must be facing Maggie Hartwell.

"Maggie, it's great to see you," Beth said, then paused, hoping for a sign that her guess was accurate.

Maggie flashed a triumphant look in the direction of the pudgy man following a couple of steps behind her.

"See I do remember everyone. Beth and I used to play volleyball together. Do you remember, Beth? Gawd, I loved high school sports."

Maggie dragged a girl forward, holding her as if anticipating an escape attempt.

"Meet Jessie, my daughter. She starts high school next fall. Doesn't have much interest in sports though. Not like me. I teach physical education. How about you? Gawd, I haven't seen so many people at one of these ever—the twentieth must be real special. Are lots of kids coming? Jessie thinks she'll be bored."

Beth inhaled deeply, as she smiled at the blushing young girl. Jessie's teeth pushed forward, their metal tips escaping lips that didn't quite close. Her gaping mouth, combined with her weak chin reminded Beth of a baby bird.

"We have twenty teens registered, and the mall has enough going on to keep you busy for days."

A flood of colour spread to the girl's hairline. Wanting to ease Jessie's discomfort at being the focus of attention, Beth turned back to the mother.

In her hour of staffing the registration desk, Beth had remembered something relevant about each newcomer, but she remembered nothing about this Maggie. Attempting to cover her failure, Beth indicated her companion at the registration table.

"Do you remember Dawn Richards?" she asked.

With a sideways glance, Maggie nodded toward the skinny woman sitting at Beth's side. "I thought it must be you, though you've lost a pile of weight, right?"

Dawn's smile tightened, but she inclined her bony chin, regally acknowledging Maggie's pronouncement.

Resting her hands on the table, Maggie crowded into Beth's comfort zone as she proclaimed, "We just loved the committee's decision to have the reunion here."

Beth drew back to allow her eardrum a respite.

Maggie lowered her voice a decibel. "Sorry. Comes from yelling instructions to teams playing half a field away. Like I was saying, it's hard to find quality time to spend with my daughter and with her being at such a vital age, I begrudge stealing a whole weekend. But when West Edmonton Mall was mentioned, I called straight away and reserved the Igloo Room. I know we're going to have the best time."

"Well, don't delay taking in the sights," Beth said, relieved that her suggested locale was a hit with someone.

To Edmontonians, a mention of the Mall brought memories of visitors desperate to find a store they had left only minutes before, but which seemed to have disappeared. It meant tantrums when retrieving kids from Red's Rec Room, the Waterpark or Galaxyland. But tourists loved the place, and teen girls loved shopping and theatres, so Beth knew Jessie would have a good time.

"You're the first of the families to check in, but soon you'll find some kids to enjoy the attractions with."

"Of course she will," Maggie said. "Everyone likes Jessie. Right Rollie?"

The man standing behind Maggie nodded.

Beth flipped through the envelopes containing information packages. Part way through she read the name Hamelin. She glanced at Dawn, their gazes met, but Dawn quickly looked away.

Beth pulled out Maggie's registration package.

"This contains your name tags and a schedule of all the planned activities. There are passes for the attractions package you picked, a map of the mall, and a list of the attendees with their room numbers. If you want, you can also have Guest Services download the mall map onto your Palm PDA."

"I'm not high tech. We'll let chance be our guide." Maggie stepped backward, restoring breathing room Beth hadn't realized she was missing.

Then, Maggie spread her arms wide. "Damn Beth, stand up. I just have to hug you."

Beth felt a moment of panic as she sank into Maggie's feather-pillow bosom. Maggie released her, then crammed the envelope into her shoulder bag and headed toward the elevators that led to Europa Boulevard.

"How the heck did you recognize her," Dawn asked in a husky whisper. "She's as big as a whale and that purple pant suit is hideous. Am I remembering wrong or was she always the skinniest kid in our class?"

Beth let Dawn's words skim by her as she flipped through the envelopes. Her stomach twisted when she reached Wade Hamelin's.

"We have a lull. How about more coffee?" Dawn grabbed her water bottle and Beth's coffee cup. Her charm bracelet jangled as she jumped to her feet.

Beth grabbed Dawn's twig-thin arm. "Why is there a package for him?"

Dawn plopped into her chair. She pried Beth's fingers from her arm. "He had every right to register."

"We agreed not to send him an invitation."

"No one did."

"How did he find out; he's been out of touch forever." Beth's hands curled into fists.

"It's just bad luck. No one wanted him here and not just because of what happened. You may not have noticed, being in his inner circle, but he enjoyed hurting people. Anyone who wasn't a cheerleader or a jock was fair game."

Beth fought her anger into submission. "When were you going to tell me?"

"I wasn't. The others thought you might not run into each other—I figured you might welcome a flash from the past."

Beth stared at the stick thin woman. Maybe bleaching her hair to that awful straw colour had short-circuited her compassion? Perhaps the miles she ran while toning her thighs had jogged loose her common sense?

Dawn's expression was tinged with evil satisfaction. She knew she'd pulled off a nine on the Richter Scale of Surprises.

Beth looked around the room, hoping for enlightenment. Arnie Hancock avoided looking at her as he chewed on his bushy mustache. As organizing committee chairman he had to be part of the conspiracy. They knew she would avoid Wade even if it meant skipping the reunion she had helped organize, so they had kept silent.

"What fantasy led you to think every second person I met wouldn't tell me?"

Dawn focused on the figure eight she was tracing on the table covering.

"The committee decided we couldn't send his cheque back because he's part of our graduating class and turning him away would be rude." Beth detected venom in her tone.

The yell of frustration rising in Beth's throat stalled when Dawn's nervous glance reminded her of their audience.

"Damn," Beth said, before flashing what she hoped was a welcoming smile at the trio of women advancing on their table.

The slender redhead in the middle of the three wore designer jeans, cinched by a leather belt with a silver buckle. The swaying of her narrow hips was accentuated by the high heels of her cowboy boots.

She said something to the plump brunette on her right and the trio looked toward the registration table and giggled. When they recovered from their outburst, the red-haired woman hugged the matronly woman on her left.

This time Beth didn't need to search her memory for names. These three had clung to each other throughout high school. Suzanne, their ringleader, had little concern for decorum, feared none of the teachers and routinely received top marks without opening a book. Obviously she hadn't changed, though she was a senior partner in a law firm and heading for a judgeship. She was also the married mother of two pre-teens whom she had not registered for the reunion.

Katy Starr, the woman on Suzanne's right had a puff of red hair surrounding her plump face. She wore her double chin and apple shape comfortably. The top of her head reached Suzanne's shoulder, but only with the help of three-inch platform heels. Katy taught life skills to special needs students. Physical disabilities plagued her son and multiple sclerosis kept her husband confined to a wheel chair.

Rhonda Peters was covered from her flat chest to her matronly hips in a gorgeous shawl woven from multiple shades of mauve wool. A cascade of colourful necklaces gave her a gypsy air suitable to her career as a weaver and artist. Rhonda, married to a well-known photographer, travelled to art and craft shows across Canada.

The camaraderie among the women pulled Beth's thoughts toward her own group of school friends, especially Jasmine. She shoved the offending envelope back amongst the others.

She leaned toward Dawn and whispered, "Does Jasmine know?" Then focusing on the advancing trio, Beth widened her welcoming smile and waited for Dawn's reply.

"Why would I tell her?"

"It was her sister who died; she needs to know," Beth said, keeping her voice low.

"Dawn. You look wonderful. That diet I recommended worked miracles. Or should I congratulate Lionel for keeping you on a fitness regime?" Suzanne's smile was warm and wide, but Dawn's remained merely polite.

A floral perfume tickled its way into Beth's nose. She fought back a sneeze.

An elegant gold watch emerged from Suzanne's sleeve as she waved her arm to encompass the banquet room. "Everything is just perfect. The committee has performed above and beyond this year."

"Suzanne Riter, right?" Dawn asked. "Your group made the reunion again this year—that's great."

"Who lost their mind and made it a family thing?" Suzanne asked. "We ignored the suggestion and left our kids and husbands at home. This is my holiday with the girls."

"But the mall is perfect for families," Dawn said.

Beth felt her eyes widen. Dawn had been the most vocal opponent to including families.

Beth reached for the box of registration packages hoping to hurry the group on their way, but Dawn tugged the box from her hands and started flipping through the envelopes.

Suzanne waved her orange-tipped fingers toward her companions. "Whatever. But poor Katy needs a break from her family responsibilities."

Katy shoved her hands deep into the pockets of her navy slacks. A strand of hair drooped across her forehead.

Dawn kept her attention on the envelopes as she muttered, "Not all of us want to shed our lives and run from our loved ones. I for one am happy with my present life."

Suzanne looked around, her smile widening as she asked, "Lionel isn't attending?"

"No," Dawn gave an audible sigh.

"What about your little boy?"

"He's with his dad in Toronto right now."

"Right, that little drug thing affected your custody fight."

"That was a lie. Besides, it's none of your business."

"Half the members of the gym went into mourning when Lionel married you. But he swears he'll tend my needs forever."

Dawn glared, but said nothing.

Suzanne turned her attention toward Beth. "You're Beth McKinney, right? I like your short hair. Naturally curly is such a pain when it's long, isn't it? Have you ever considered adding some red highlights?

"I caught your picture on the news after Lisette Dorrien was murdered. I was on a committee with her once, very stand-offish. Mind you, with the stories circulating about her husband, I was monstrously relieved I'd had nothing to do with her. You can't be too careful with your reputation when you're climbing the ladder to the Supreme Court. You're a librarian, right? Still single I suppose, or are you a modern woman who has stuck with her maiden name? Do you have kids? I should know all this, but keeping up with everyone is impossible. The only time I hear from some people is when they get married again. I think just the three of us are with our original spouses."

Beth shook her head. "No husband either."

"She's engaged." Dawn offered the tidbit as if it somehow changed Beth's condition from terminal to treatable.

"Anyone we know?"

"I'm afraid not," Beth answered.

"When do we meet him?" Rhonda asked, causing Suzanne to glare at her for interrupting.

"Mike should be at the banquet," Beth said, crossing her fingers.

"Here you go." Dawn shoved the envelopes toward the women. "All the scheduled activities are detailed."

"Don't worry about us. We know how to make our own fun." Suzanne followed her comment with a wink as she led the trio toward the crowd gathered around the refreshments table.

Katy veered away from Suzanne as they approached the group and sauntered toward the wall of photos.

"Suzanne is a real bitch in heat. She's always trying to tempt Lionel away from me. Just watch. She'll pick up some guy to party with," Dawn whispered. "She's lucky she hasn't taken a nasty surprise home to that original husband of hers."

"I don't care about Suzanne's habits, or anyone else's either. I've got to get to Jasmine before she hears about Wade."

"So now it's not about an old flame, but about Jasmine's sensitivities?" Dawn raised her eyebrows. "I wouldn't be that compassionate about someone who wouldn't talk to me for ten years."

"We're friends again."

"Of course you are. So, which is it? Fear that Jasmine will take a knife to him, or that you'll fall into his arms?"

Beth was repelled by the thought of Wade, the first in her long line of romantic disasters. She wanted to protect Jasmine, not worry about what was biting Dawn's bottom.

A familiar figure glided down the hall toward them. Beth waved and called out, "Gina."

"Yes, it is about Jasmine," Beth told Dawn. "Reinforcements have just arrived."

CHAPTER THREE

Gina's two-piece silk suit clung where it was supposed to and swayed gently everywhere else. Its grey waterfall pattern yelled designer.

Beth remembered the dress Mike had said looked extraordinary on her. She wished she'd bought it instead of opting for serviceable, comfortable, and boring. Well, it was too late now.

As Gina glided along the hallway toward them, the hem of her skirt swayed against her dedicated marathoner's calves. The obsidian shine of her hair and her slightly oval eyes added to the impression that she was a foreign movie star disguised as Beth's friend.

After several steps her faintly arrogant expression relaxed into a delighted smile that showed teeth and deepened her dimples.

"Beth, damn, I was betting you'd skip out, even if you were on the organizing committee. So what's your escape plan?"

As Beth walked around the table to hug her friend, she wished Wade's attendance did give her a credible reason to escape.

"You look great," Beth said.

"I should look a hell of a lot better than that," Gina said with a sideways glance toward Dawn. Her grin lit a mischievous gleam in her eyes. "Attending one of these reunions, especially the landmark twenty-year gala, has to involve intensive dieting, hours of aerobics, maybe a tuck or two, and of course the right clothes. The least you can offer is that I look fabulous darling."

Beth noted the flick of Gina's wrist, the forward thrust of her skeletal hip bones, and the mocking tone of her dreadfully overdone accent. She cringed knowing Gina was alluding to Dawn's transformation from a divorcee who jiggled when she walked, to a newlywed with a killer body. Dawn's horrified expression said she'd hit a bull's eye.

Careful to keep her expression neutral, Beth said, "You do look fabulous, but I suppose you just missed lunch and grabbed something from the back of your closet, and with that minuscule effort have managed to shine."

Gina shrugged. "Close. I should have missed lunch—airport food is so relentlessly healthy. I flew straight in from London after ten days of fighting with our Japanese suppliers. Even family connections didn't smooth my path to that deal. Worse yet, family dinners over there aren't big on meat. I might murder a cow myself if it meant a juicy steak dinner."

"Should we be honoured you've made time for us?"

"This is my vacation. So I'm all yours unless a major deal drops dead or I'm promoted to CEO."

Beth smiled at Gina's grandiose statements, but knew every word she uttered was true.

Gina scanned the conference room. Beth turned to follow her gaze. The grey tones seemed depressingly ordinary, the dusty rose accents passé. The scattering of circular tables were impersonal hotel meeting room decor. Even the institution-sized coffee urn, that had seemed so important, looked like a glaring mistake.

The blue-on-blue poster boldly displaying their Mosquette Academy motto looked like the cardboard cut out that it was. The blue ribbons, balloons, and streamers surrounding it yelled high school. The memorabilia tables, cluttered with items pulled from boxes and drawers once every five years, lay in disarray. Beth shuddered.

"Food—donuts yet," Gina said. "Make way ladies, I'm ravenous."

Beth pulled Gina closer. "We've got to talk first. There's a crisis and I need your help."

Gina squinted. Beth wondered if she was wearing her contacts. "I only deal with work-related crises or maybe kid crises, though that area of my life has slowed to an occasional plea for money."

"It's about Wade."

Gina grabbed Beth's hands and twirled her in an excited dance. "Did I tell you I ran into him in Bali? He manages a hotel there. Still skirt crazy, but he has perfected that Caribbean pirate look that drives me wild. Said he was thinking of moving back to Canada."

A tiny butterfly of dread fluttered in Beth's stomach. She clutched the edge of the table. "Did you tell him about the reunion?"

Gina's excitement deflated. "I told him I expected to see him here. And suggested he use the visit to check out job prospects in person."

Beth noticed Dawn's avid interest. The overall noise level seemed to have dropped, as if ears, not tongues, were working.

"You still have a thing for him," Gina said. "After all this time. Look we had some fun, but if it bothers you, I'll dump him."

"All I want is his absence. Jasmine will be here."

"Hell, I talked to Jasmine about him, maybe a year ago, and she said she'd like to meet up with him. One of her shrinks probably told her to deal with that hurt so she can get on with her life."

"I doubt this is the time or place."

Gina shrugged. "She's gone through two more divorces than I have, so something is working against her eternal search for happiness. If it's Wade, why not let them duel until their history is dead?"

"Does she know he's coming?"

Gina wagged her finger. "Leading the horse to water isn't always the easy part. Get them together; let the chemistry work. A little incendiary excitement can only enliven a party."

Beth remembered Gina being the butt of jokes, not the instigator. Throughout high school, her outspoken opinions had drawn advocates and opponents in equal proportions. Teachers loved her. Some of the students admired her, but others, like Wade and his fellow jocks, had sneered. Beth remembered the distress she'd felt because one of her best friends and her boyfriend hated each other.

That had obviously changed; Beth preferred the

hatred. Still, Gina was probably right about Jasmine, and Beth knew her caustic observations could be applied to them all.

Jasmine may have had three bad marriages, but Beth had none—good or bad. She thought she could trust Mike, but there had been others who had betrayed her love.

"Come on Beth, brighten up. You're engaged now. Jasmine has her daughter and from what I hear, a great prospect in the romance department—one with looks, money, and political aspirations. Think of Wade's arrival as a chance to reformat your memory chips."

Beth took the envelope Dawn was clutching and handed it to Gina.

"Itinerary?" Gina inquired, her expression restored to good humour. She rested her hand on Beth's forearm. "Relax old girl, all will be fine, providing I get my donut fix. What say we meet in the Fantasy Lounge at four o'clock and really talk? Will Trista be here by then?"

"Yes, but Jasmine won't arrive until around six."

"What about Mike? Do I finally get to meet your mystery man?"

Beth checked her watch. It was too early for Mike to leave work, but she longed to return to her room and find him waiting. He would take her concerns seriously. Then he would tease her back to her usual competent self. "He should be here soon, at least I haven't heard otherwise."

"You don't keep a close eye on him?"

"Not Mike. Even if it was possible, it would be unnecessary."

CHAPTER FOUR

"Don't be so complacent about your fellow. All men need watching," Dawn said as they watched Gina stroll toward a table laden with food and drink. "There's always a Gina, or a Suzanne, waiting to pounce and it's in a guy's nature to respond."

"If you think that, maybe you married the wrong guy."

"Lionel is surrounded by half-naked women all day. I make sure he has equally enticing scenery when he gets home."

"You work out daily?"

"We exercise together."

"He has an excellent rep as a trainer."

"And if he's a good boy, I might buy him a gym of his own one day."

Beth's cellphone chimed. She pulled it from her jacket pocket. Such power in so tiny an instrument; still, next month she was trading it in for one of the next generation.

Mike's number showed on the call display. Damn, something was going to delay him. Not that she was pushing him to meet her old friends. Mike had encouraged her to join the organizing committee. He wanted to know everything going on in her life, past and present, and he said he wanted to be a major part of her future.

"Dad had a stroke. He's in hospital, so I'm heading

for Saskatchewan. I'll stop by to pick you up."

The reunion committee would understand she needed to help Mike cope with his father's illness. They would simply have to handle everything without her.

Beth stared at the banner stretched across the entrance. She had failed Jasmine once before, she couldn't do it again. By attending, Wade had made skipping the reunion impossible.

"I can't go with you. There's a crisis here that I have to deal with."

"What's happened?"

She outlined the situation and hoped he would understand. "Jasmine needs my help and after working so hard to re-establish our friendship, I can't abandon her."

"Jasmine can manage without you."

Beth felt a headache menacing the base of her skull. He should know she wanted to go with him, to share his pain. But, this one time, he had to understand that someone else needed her more than he did.

"I can't help your dad, but I can support Jasmine."

"You would be helping me."

Dawn's pixie ears seemed to perk up as she gathered ammunition for future gossip sessions.

Beth shrugged the tension from her shoulders. "I can't just abandon everything here. Let me get things organized, delegate my duties. Call when you get there. Let me know how he is. I'll come as soon as I know Jasmine will be all right."

Beth heard a click. Why was he pushing her? During

their first months together, she'd been certain he was the person she would spend the rest of her life with. Now he was demanding too much.

"Family crisis?" Dawn asked.

"I have to leave."

"But you're scheduled for another hour."

Beth gathered her belongings and approached Arnie Hancock. He chewed at his mustache as she explained she might have to leave the reunion before the banquet. His understanding smile disappeared when she told him to take over her shift. As committee chairman, he was as much to blame for the Wade problem as Dawn.

"Not telling me Wade was going to be here was a dirty trick. I thought you were a better person than that."

"We voted. I couldn't go against the majority."

"If you and Dawn voted against his attending, and Carl and Pete for, my vote would have been the tie breaker."

"It was three to one for and we needed your help. Dawn said you would pull out if you knew."

"That should have been my decision."

Beth pushed past him and strode toward the lobby. It was too late for anything but damage control. She would locate Trista and recruit her help with Jasmine. Trista had always been more understanding than Gina.

Rushing into the lobby, Beth spotted Lorelei, her liaison with the hotel, who had saved her sanity and the reunion countless times. She was an Australian import of Scottish ancestry and had the reddish hair and complexion to prove it.

"What's the problem, Beth?"

"Has Trista Flynn registered yet?"

Lorelei checked the computer. "About half an hour ago. Do you want me to ring her?"

Beth nodded, then waited through a half dozen rings. "She must have gone out. She hasn't checked in with your group?"

"Don't worry, I'll track her down."

"Well, remember to holler if you need me."

Beth crossed the flower-filled lobby to the elevators, planning to retreat to her room and take a pill for her headache. If only Lorelei's efficient magic could make Wade disappear—perhaps a lost room registration would do it?

As she waited, the elevator doors opened and a woman stepped out. Beth scrutinized her vaguely familiar features. She wore no nametag, so perhaps she was at the hotel for some other function. After a momentary pause, the woman flung her arms wide and clasped Beth around her shoulders.

Another anonymous hugger.

"Beth, it's wonderful to see you." The woman spoke with a slight accent, one Beth couldn't place.

Beth was embarrassed to admit she didn't have a clue about the woman's identity. Who in her class looked like a Spanish matron?

"I'm sorry," she mumbled.

"You don't recognize me, do you? I know it's been twenty years, but surely you recognize your best pal. Or does my tiny bit of Texas drawl make such a difference?"

Beth looked closely. Her hair had gone from brown to black and her eyes, that used to be plain brown, now flashed black fire as they laughed at her confusion.

Trista was dramatically different, with a new exuberance. Beth wondered whether her memory had faded with time or if some remaking had taken place.

The "Yellow Rose of Texas" rang through the lobby, interrupting her apology.

"I should have turned that off," Trista said. She reached inside her shoulder bag and pulled out a rather large, old-fashioned cellphone. She frowned as she studied the call display.

"Go ahead," Beth said.

Trista pressed the talk button. "Hello." She listened for a moment, then glanced at Beth and turned away. The mirrors lining the lobby walls showed the ferocity of her expression.

"Not here, not now, never." She abruptly disconnected the call. Her smile had returned when she again faced Beth, but it looked forced.

"A student with a problem."

"I was looking for you," Beth said.

Trista regained her enthusiasm and linked arms with Beth. "I can register later. I spotted a lounge just off the lobby. Let's get some coffee and catch up."

"Am I that obvious?"

"Yes, you are."

They slid the upholstered tub chairs close to the small table. The pensive high school friend Beth remembered had emerged. Trista had been the one who drifted near the edge of a conversation gathering facts and impressions.

"Wade is attending the reunion."

Trista looked at Beth for a moment. Her brow wrinkled into a puzzled frown. It seemed impossible she had forgotten Wade, but as Beth gathered her thoughts to explain further, Trista's eyes narrowed.

"That bastard," she said, staring absently at the cellphone lying on the table beside her. She placed her hand on Beth's shoulder. "Of course, you don't want to see him."

"It's not me I'm concerned about—it's Jasmine. She can't want to meet him. Even if she does, I don't think this is the right place."

Trista tilted her head. "If it's not going to bother you to see him, considering that you were an item for what—nearly three years—why should she be so shook up?"

"He did kill her sister."

"So the guy is scum. He always was. But don't worry about Jasmine, she's a survivor."

Trista's piercing stare made Beth uncomfortable. Beth knew any pronouncement that followed would be insightful. Gina used to swear Trista had gypsy ancestors.

"I think this is about you," Trista said. "You aren't over Wade."

"My relationship with Wade isn't part of this. What we had is history."

"History is relevant, especially at our age. Everything we do is to atone for some old sin or to prepare us for the final judgement call."

"I see you haven't grown less morbid." Beth caught herself before she said more.

"Why haven't we met in all this time?" Beth asked, steering the conversation toward neutral ground. "I've seen Gina three or four times and Jasmine more often than that. But I haven't seen you since the summer we graduated."

"Just too busy teaching those young Texas maidens how to be good people. It takes more effort than I can muster to get back to the cold country."

"You could have joined us in Mexico."

"I prefer spending my vacations in museums rather than on tourist infested beaches."

Beth sipped her coffee and searched for more to say. It seemed to her there should be hours of catching up to do, but her thoughts were stuck on Wade and Jasmine.

Trista put down her cup. "Beth, I understand your reluctance, but stop obsessing about him. Don't let him spoil the first time our group has been together since graduation."

Her distant look returned, and Beth wondered what she was thinking.

"I'm afraid Jasmine will leave when she hears Wade is coming," Beth said.

"Why give her such little credit?" Trista said, her voice sharp with anger. "Do you really think she'd miss spending time with us, just because some jerk chooses to reappear?"

Beth sat her cup on the table and leaned back in her chair. She pressed her fingertips together, trying to keep her voice even. "Gina thinks meeting Wade will be good therapy for Jasmine. She blames all three failed marriages on unresolved problems arising from Sharon's death."

The "Yellow Rose of Texas" played again. Trista flipped open the phone. With a quick glance at the call display her anger poured into the receiver. "My answer is no. Don't phone again." She switched it off and shoved it into her purse.

Beth's curiosity overflowed. "Is there a problem?" she asked.

"I'll handle it." Trista shifted, tugging at the hem of her emerald green skirt. "One of my students wants an extension for an assignment. Every year I have to train them not to phone me with their problems."

"You don't give them your cellphone number, do you?"

"There's very little you can keep secret on that damned Internet. Of course you know that, you teach people to dig up secrets."

Beth stared at her. Certainly, she tutored people in online investing and money management, and at the library she compiled information about businesses, but to accuse her of accessing secrets was ludicrous. She regretted all the years when they'd had no contact. If Trista knew her better, she would realize Beth would never invade the privacy of another person.

"Until I taught a course in computer ethics last term, I didn't realize what the privacy advocates were talking about." Trista clutched her skirt, squeezing the fabric tight against her thighs. She jumped up and grabbed her purse. "I better go register. We'll talk more later."

"I'm meeting Gina here at four. Come join us," Beth called toward her retreating back.

CHAPTER FIVE

The stretch of asphalt seemed to extend forever. A flat road in a flat land required little of Mike's powers of concentration to keep his truck pointed east. The thump of a sad country song flowed from the radio.

Two terrible things had happened to him today. What would be the third? First, the call saying his father had suffered a stroke, a bad one, but so far not deadly. Then Beth's refusal to come with him.

He shouldn't be surprised that she had found another reason to avoid meeting his family. She was a privacy nut. What he knew about her had come in a broken trail of need-to-know vignettes. He remembered the blankness in her father's eyes when they were introduced, and how Beth had blushed when he told her father they had been dating for nearly a year.

Since then, he had come to know and like her family, but she had constantly avoided meeting his. It had taken a second year before she agreed to marry him. In the months since then, she had changed the topic every time he suggested setting a date.

He knew she was nervous about the reunion. She desperately wanted it to succeed and had spent months perfecting every damn detail. She excelled at anything she touched. She made more money than he did and had a hell of a lot more education too.

Still, she had the reunion under control. Every person

knew their assigned tasks. For once, she could have ranked him tops on her list of priorities, but no, someone else needed her, so again he was pushed aside.

Who were these people to take priority? Most she hadn't seen in twenty years. What did that say about her? He had missed a few of his high school reunions but rarely and always for good reason. She had missed every single one and that was no coincidence. Why was she so determined to attend this one?

The fields on either side of the divided four-lane highway were brown with stubble, ready for their white winter covering. In hollows and shady places snow already gathered, giving the landscape a speckled look. A coyote trotted across the open prairie, ignoring the highway traffic. The few clusters of trees encircling farm buildings had long since shed their greenery, leaving only dead fingers reaching toward a scattering of flat motionless clouds.

He punched a string of numbers on his cellphone, a high-tech toy Beth had given him on the one-year anniversary of their first meeting—a ghoulish anniversary to mark, as it was also the day a mutual friend had died.

He twisted the radio dial, turning the country music lower as his brother's voice came through the receiver telling him they would call back later if he left a message. He dialed the hospital.

He had known the nurse who answered all his life, even dated her when he was teaching school, before she married and before he changed careers. She greeted him like they had seen each other yesterday and assured him his dad was getting expert care. Then she paged John. That friendliness was a perk of small town living. People knew everyone and their brother, and weren't too busy to track them down for you.

John didn't show the same optimism as the nurse had, maybe because their uncle had died of a massive stroke only months earlier. He reported that the doctor had been guarded about their father's condition, though getting him to the hospital early gave him the benefit of a new treatment that promised to reverse much of the damage.

John said he was sorry Beth couldn't make it, but that he understood. Mike heard disapproval in his voice.

What right did John have to judge Beth for her absence? She had a life of her own. Mike stared at the empty highway trying to ignore the question goading him: Did she want him to be part of it?

CHAPTER SIX

Beth decided she would have known Harvey McIntosh anywhere. He was still the shortest man in the room and though slender, he was chunkier than the mouse of a boy she remembered. He had obviously spent a fortune on his casual sweater and slacks, though the ease with which he wore them said he hadn't bought them solely for the reunion.

Harvey stood at the centre of a group, yet when she entered the meeting room he looked in her direction and waved. With a word to the others, he walked toward her.

Beth clenched her fists in her jacket pockets. Harvey had become her friend the first day of kindergarten; they had spent the following years sharing emotions, dissecting people's lives, and speculating on their destinies. She once thought he would make a good rabbi, but since he wasn't Jewish, psychiatry fit him just as well.

His hand was warm and his grip firm enough to convey strength without being overpowering. She felt her shoulders relax, surprised at the tension generated by meeting an old friend. Perhaps her fear came from meeting an old friend who was also an analyst?

"Beth, you don't disappoint," Harvey said tilting his head and smiling up at her, making her feel she had more than two inches on him.

She felt flustered and extended her hand. "It's been forever."

"I always had a crush on you." He shook his head, smiling at the reminiscence. "I'm glad to see I had great taste even as a timid adolescent."

Beth felt her face grow warm. His greeting was certainly superior to the standard, 'you look great' or 'you haven't changed' comments she'd been fielding for most of the afternoon.

"You know just what to say to make a woman's day."

"Though, maybe you're a little sadder," he continued.

So he'd heard about the day's events. She flashed back to times when they'd met over fries and pop in the mall, with Harvey probing her for the details of her latest crisis, her denying there was anything to probe.

"Not sadder," she defended her mood. "Just more familiar with life's twists and turns."

Harvey's grin turned upside-down in concentration. "You always did take life too seriously."

"So you were analyzing people back then too?"

He shrugged. "Are you upset about Wade being here?"

She saw the weekend stretching before her as a long interrogation about her feelings and wished she had run away with Mike. Beth met Harvey's look of concern with an equally solemn one. "People should stop worrying about me."

"You took twenty years to get to a reunion. No one wants you scared away."

"It was never convenient to attend."

"Really?"

"I lived in Toronto for nearly half of that time."

"Excuses."

"Valid reasons."

"Whatever. You're here now. What can I do to keep you here?"

"Keep Wade away from Jasmine and me."

"That's the plan."

Beth looked at his compassionate smile, then beyond him to the groups scattered around the room. Several people smiled and nodded. One fellow gave her a thumbs-up. She was surrounded by surrogate parents.

God, half the people in the room even looked like her parents. What was she worrying about? Wade probably had a belly and only half of his thick black hair. He wouldn't be the handsome, arrogant Wade of her memories.

"I'm engaged now," Beth pointed out, hoping to prove she was a whole person capable of surviving a chance meeting with an old boyfriend.

"I'm looking forward to meeting your fiancé. Will he arrive before tomorrow's banquet?"

"He's been called away. His father is ill."

Harvey's eyes widened and his right eyebrow rose. "You have grown up. I remember when you would have used a broken nail as an excuse to avoid a confrontation."

All they needed was a couch and a notebook to make the session official.

"Or are we the lesser evil?"

"I'm my own woman, no man dictates my life."

"And which man isn't dictating this weekend? Wade or your fiancé? Remember, successful relationships require flexibility."

"Shall I phone for a follow-up session?"

"Relax. I'm kidding you. From what I hear, you've found a good person this time."

"I'm meeting Trista and Gina in the Fantasy Lounge," Beth said as she made a production of looking at her watch. It was only three-thirty. "I'm already late."

Harvey's smile told her that he knew she was lying. Damn, did everyone know her business?

"How about we meet for breakfast tomorrow, around ten-thirty, and talk about old times," Harvey said as he retreated a step and raised his hand in a Scout salute. "I promise, no lectures or psychoanalysis, just old-fashioned gossip."

"You already know everything about me."

"And I promise I'll know all the facts, rumours, and speculation about every one of our classmates."

"All right. Ten-thirty in the lobby. I'm meeting the organizing committee at nine-thirty and if I can't keep them on track I might be late."

"You're never late."

CHAPTER SEVEN

Harvey watched Beth walk away. She still carried herself like an athlete. Of course, with parents who owned a fitness centre and a mother who was a personal trainer she had lots of incentive. He preferred women who looked healthy and at 5'6" with nice curves, she fit that description. He was glad she had resisted plastering on makeup. Her high cheekbones didn't need artificial help.

He thought her taste in clothes had changed, but the stylish wool of her plain beige dress suited her. Her scarf and elaborate pin added a colourful touch.

She was tense, though. It showed in her stiff shoulders and rigid stance and in the stress that he picked up in her voice. Passing responsibilities to her was natural because you knew she would accomplish everything and then some. When this reunion was over she would probably relax; until then, Harvey figured he had best watch her for signs of collapse.

He had mixed feelings about Wade's reappearance. Wade Hamelin liked picking on the weak of any species, as Harvey knew only too well. Wade and his gang of jocks had been the reason he'd dropped all competitive sports. He had hated their constant short jokes, cruel barbs about his divorced parents, and taunts that he was a sissy for hanging out with girls.

His days had become worse when Beth started dating

Wade. Beth had pushed him aside, even as Wade threatened physical damage.

Though high school had been torture, it had spurred him toward helping others surmount problems. Wasn't that what shrinks did?

Now Beth needed him. She might think she had control of her life, but Harvey knew she was wrong. She had the usual trappings of success, the big house, the sports car, cash to set her parents up in a fitness club, and enough left over to indulge her wanderlust.

But only her family and her two cats were permanent fixtures in her life. Harvey knew she wasn't a hermit, but she had been leery of trusting anyone since their graduation.

Harvey didn't feel guilty about collecting every scrap of gossip he heard about Beth or about instigating conversations when facts weren't volunteered. He knew about her string of men friends, each less eligible than the last, each easier for her to drop. Until now. This last fellow might be different but maybe she saw something negative in him, too. Something she could worry into a reason to flee.

When he heard Beth was attending the reunion, he'd toyed with the idea of pursuing her, just like in his high school dreams. Now he saw that she hadn't put Wade behind her.

Not that any of them had. He had tried to forget the night of the accident, but it remained in sharp focus. Even before public education campaigns against drunk driving, Beth had been smart enough to try to grab the keys from Wade's hand. Unsuccessful, she had refused to ride with him. The others in their group should have tackled him instead of standing around.

None of them imagined that Wade would see Jasmine's sister, Sharon, on her way home from work, would offer her a ride, would run a red light and collide with a fully loaded truck. Sharon, thrown through the windshield, had her throat slashed and then her head crushed when she hit the curb. And what particular devil had led their cheerful group to the site only minutes after the accident?

Jasmine had scrambled from the car, screaming when she recognized her sister through the coating of blood and brain tissue. Beth had watched Wade have a cut on his hand bandaged. It took ten years and an accidental meeting halfway around the world for Beth and Jasmine to begin to heal the rift.

Harvey blinked away his tears. After the tragedy, most of their class drew closer, but not Beth and her three friends. Jasmine had married a guy ten years older than her within months of the accident and divorced him soon after their daughter was born. She tried marriage twice more, with equally bad results.

Trista had fled to the States and closeted herself with her college studies. Then, she found work in Texas at a posh school for the daughters of the rich and famous. She never married; only the advent of e-mail had nudged her back into the circle of her classmates.

Gina was another victim of the trauma of that night. She had moved around Canada and the States for years, marrying young, then abandoning custody of her two children to her husband. Her escapades were gossiped about at length. The latest being how she had met Wade, seduced him and invited him to the reunion. Dawn had wasted no time spreading that morsel.

This reunion marked the first time the five of them would be together in twenty years, and Wade had to intrude. Harvey wondered what role Dawn had played in escalating the uproar. She had been a troublemaker since grade school.

A heavy fist punched into Harvey's shoulder, jolting him from his reverie. He smiled and turned to face Joe Small, a gigantic ex-football player who was fighting a battle against alcoholism.

Time to mingle.

CHAPTER EIGHT

Gina and Trista were already in the lounge when Beth arrived. Trista held a brandy snifter. Gina's glass contained something over ice.

High glass walls cut down the constant rumble and roar from the mall, so the room felt like a dim hiding place. Beth pulled out a chair and met their concerned expressions with a deep sigh.

"If I ever volunteer to help with something like this reunion again, just commit me straight away."

"It's great seeing everyone though, isn't it?"

Beth slipped off her leather pumps and wiggled her toes. "I should have worn sensible shoes."

"Never do that girl," Gina said, as she sipped her drink. "I rely on a short skirt, shapely legs, and agonizingly high heels to give me an advantage. Mind you, in my field, the men may be rich and powerful, but most of them are shy computer nerds. It's a match made in my favour."

Gina always had played to an audience, even when there was no one to fully appreciate her allure.

Trista stretched her legs and studied the black suede flats she was wearing. "Only someone who spends the entire day on their feet can appreciate well-crafted footwear."

"You only have a horde of teenage girls to impress. I have deprived males pretending not to notice." Gina raised her glass high in the air. "A toast to all the sexual harassment decisions that allow us to flaunt without fear of repercussions."

After sipping her drink, she looked at Trista intently. "How you've managed to live like a nun for so long, I'll never understand."

"My girls are tough critics."

"Isn't it all uniforms with your crowd?"

"You'd be surprised what a fifteen-year-old can do with a uniform."

"It's the lack of men I couldn't stand."

"That always was your problem, Gina."

Gina stuck her tongue out in Trista's direction. Beth leaned back in her chair. The women had always been opposites. The only thing they had in common was their friendship with her.

"Remember the summer before Grade 12? We spent it sunbathing at Mill Creek Swimming Pool," Beth said.

"I haven't talked that much in the twenty years since," Trista said. "I've been too busy to find friends like you guys."

"You had a crush on Harvey. Nothing ever developed?" Beth asked.

"I'd forgotten that."

"I saw him this afternoon. He's still cute."

"I'm content with my life as it is," Trista said.

"Hell, you don't know what you've missed," Gina interjected. "There's nothing like the right man and a couple of kids to fill you to overflowing with love and joy."

Beth met Trista's gaze, then both stared at Gina in disbelief.

"I didn't say it was everything or for me, but when I see my kids with their dad and stepmom, I know that touchy feely stuff exists."

"Is Harvey unattached?" Trista asked.

"Maybe you should ask him," Beth suggested.

"He's a psychologist."

"You're a teacher. It's a match made in heaven."

"Maybe I will, if I run into him."

"Any of the teachers here yet?" Gina asked.

"Miss McKay."

"Remember the first day of Grade 12 science? She had first-year-teacher written all over her even though she was trying so hard to look mature."

"I remember her suit and prim hair style. She looked like a kid wearing mom's clothes."

"She still looks younger than the rest of us, but now she dresses like a teenager."

"Beth, she started dressing like that about three months into the year—around the time she started hitting on the senior boys," Gina said.

"She didn't!"

"You were too wrapped up in Wade to notice the competition. The rest of us poor damsels knew only too well that she was sexy and available."

Gina's words broke the spell, and Beth sat a little straighter in her chair.

"Oh, quit looking so devastated at the mention of his name. Sharon's death was a stupid accident—that's life."

"You're right," Trista said, her voice resonating with assurance. "I bet we've all had just as bad, maybe even worse things happen to us since."

"Have you?" Gina leaned forward, her glass clutched in her hand. "Do tell what terrible secrets are hidden away in your nunnery."

Trista flushed, then looked toward Beth for help. "Haven't you Beth? When your parents lost their business and your friend was killed, and when that lunatic held you hostage. Those were all traumatic events."

Beth asked the waitress to bring her a glass of sherry. "As we get older, we gain experience handling disasters."

"Practice makes perfect, they say," Gina said. "Never believed that myself. Every bloody disaster is just that. Betrayal now hurts as much as it did ten years ago. The trick is coming to terms with what threatens to destroy you."

"Compromise and conciliation? Doesn't sound like a business woman," Trista said.

"I'm more the identify and destroy type. Beth is the master of avoidance. I think it would be better if you confronted your enemy and then walked away purified."

Beth couldn't help but grin at Gina's mind games. "You mean I should get over Wade and get on with my life?"

Gina's lips turned up in a triumphant smile. "Thatta girl," she said. "I knew you would come around. That's why I asked Wade to join us."

She looked toward the door of the lounge. Silence fell upon their table. When Beth saw Trista's pink cheeks fade to a sickly pallor, she twisted around, afraid of confirming her suspicions.

Wade's shoulders hadn't shrunk and his chest hadn't sunk into his belly. The stubble on his chin and his casual mop of dark hair worked with his tan. A touch of gold showed in his smile and another twinkled in his ear. As Gina had said, he looked like a swashbuckling Caribbean pirate.

Beth felt her pulse race when he grinned at her. She had always loved his lopsided smile.

Then the room faded away and she remembered street lights glaring down on a crushed vehicle, Sharon's mangled body, and a younger Wade insisting the accident was the other driver's fault.

Her first impulse was to straighten her shoulders and walk out of the room, evading his outstretched hand, ignoring the curious stares of her former classmates. Instead, she waited as he swaggered toward their table and drew out the chair next to Gina.

Beth saw trepidation hover in his eyes and felt a surge of power. One word from her would cast him out of their circle. But Gina was right: Wade was simply a boy she had known long ago.

She stretched her hand across the table, meeting his halfway.

CHAPTER NINE

Beth endured Gina's enthusiastic attempts at conversation for fifteen minutes, then excused herself and sought the privacy of her room.

Wade caught her at the elevators, and holding her elbow, hurried her inside. She tried to pull away, but he wrapped his fingers around her arm and held tight.

"It's been ages, Beth. You're still beautiful." He placed his index finger under her chin and forced her to meet his gaze. "I was hoping you looked like a house frau."

"Push the button Wade, I'm going to my room."

"I'll come with you. We've a lot to talk about."

He leaned close, moving to cage her against the wall. She spotted a tinge of grey in his chin stubble and a bit of desperation in his expression. Beth put her hands on his chest and pushed him away. She knew how to handle unwanted attention.

"Whatever was between us died twenty years ago."

"You never married, neither did I. That should tell you something."

"That you impaired my ability to love anyone?"

"That you still love me." He followed her out of the elevator, holding her arm as he looked down the hall.

She shook him loose. "I love someone else."

The scowl she remembered marred his good looks. Then he let a smile play across his lips. "Maybe I will convince you otherwise."

"Touch me again and I call security."

"Still calling Daddy for help? You and your friends think so much of yourselves, always putting on airs." Then as he turned toward the open elevator, he added, "Before this weekend is over, you'll regret rejecting me."

Beth hurried down the hall and locked herself in her suite. She studied her reflection in the mirrors that surrounded the Jacuzzi. She didn't like the timid mouse staring back at her, so she looked away, only to see the same mouse in the mirror above the dressing table. The room had too damn many mirrors.

She longed to run home, but one of her reunion jobs was to stay at the hotel as a liaison for the out-of-town attendees. She had agreed to stay on site, thinking she would have Mike to keep her company. Now she longed for her cats and the comfort of Mike's embrace.

She relaxed in one of the comfortable chairs in the sitting area that set her luxurious corner suite apart from the standard rooms, glad she hadn't succumbed to the allure of sleeping in an outrigger or a Victorian carriage.

Fantasyland Hotel's theme rooms had rapidly filled with attendees, especially those with families. Even the bridal suite had been rented by a classmate celebrating his second marriage.

Of course, the large suite had drawbacks. Dawn had designated it a suitable place to store committee records. She had also insisted they needed its privacy to discuss any problems that might arise. After her performance at the registration desk, Beth knew Dawn also wanted a place to rip people apart with no danger of eavesdroppers.

Beth looked away from the mirrors, letting her gaze drop to the spare keycard on the dresser. Mike wasn't going to claim it. She should return it to the front desk and maybe her own as well. Maybe she should run home. Maybe she should run to Saskatchewan. Dawn would call her a coward, but Mike had said he needed her.

She looked into the mirror again, studying her miserable expression. Then she looked at the photo of Mike that sat on the night table. She missed him, but staying had been her decision. She wouldn't use him as an excuse to shirk her duties.

A brisk knock on her door brought her out of her daze. She had always conquered disaster with work and smiles, and by keeping people outside the high brick wall that protected her vulnerable spots.

Trista and Gina stood in the hall. Gina, wearing a nearly frontless, mid-thigh black dress looked extremely sexy. The silver chain of a glittery black evening bag hung over her shoulder.

Trista's dress, a pale green silk with long sleeves and a demure neckline presented a dramatic contrast. She wore her dark hair in a French twist. Over her shoulder she'd slung her serviceable purse.

They smirked like kids as Gina sang out a drum roll, reached over, and pulled Jasmine into view.

"Jasmine, why didn't you call my room when you arrived?" Beth asked grasping her outstretched hands.

"Gina intercepted me. We've been talking."

Gina nodded. Beth sighed with relief. She hated breaking bad news.

"I promised to be civil to him, but that's all," Jasmine said.

"That's all Beth managed," Gina said.

Beth studied Jasmine. She was flushed and her greying hair needed to be tamed. Her eyes were surrounded by dark circles and lines of fatigue pulled at her mouth. She raised her hand to her lips and nibbled at the edge of an already mutilated fingernail.

"We were bound to meet again one day," Jasmine said. "Isn't it lovely that I will have my oldest, dearest friends to support me when it happens?"

She pulled her cotton sweater away from her generous bust, then stretched her arms to encircle them in a group hug. "I'm so happy to see you all."

Gina pulled away first and stepped into the room. "Wade promised to keep his distance tonight."

"Seeing him again was a shock." Beth motioned the others to follow Gina into the room.

"We're going to dinner," Trista said, twisting the strap of her heavy purse between her hands. "You are going to come, aren't you?"

"Duty calls, so yes, I will be at dinner."

"Are you sure you're up to it?" Trista asked, as she snatched up the picture Beth had propped against the base of the bedside lamp. "Is this Mike?" she asked.

Beth felt herself flush. "I took it during our hiking trip near Jasper."

"You must look great together," Gina said, as she squinted at the photo. "Doesn't look like your usual shallow, self-centred type."

"I've changed my criteria. If Mike has a fault, it's working to keep everybody he knows safe." And maybe being a bit controlling, she thought disloyally.

"Are you wearing that?" Gina asked as she drifted about the room, stopping to pull back the drapes and check the view.

Her tone left little doubt that Beth needed to change into her own version of a slinky black dress.

"Never mind her, Beth, your dress is darling," Jasmine said, following Gina's path to the window, then retracing her steps to study her reflection in the mirror above the dresser. "I'm just down the hall. Give me ten minutes to shower off that boring five-hour drive from Lethbridge. If Hollis could see me now, he might reconsider our wedding. The last thing a politician needs is a wife who doesn't travel well."

Beth had already entered the bathroom. As she closed the door she said, "Help yourselves to the bar. It'll take me just a minute to change."

CHAPTER TEN

"I love everything," Jasmine said as they stood in the doorway of the meeting room where arrangements of mums and sunflowers decorated the linen covered tables.

Beth inhaled the mixed aroma of garlic and olive oil coming from the pasta fiesta buffet.

"Lorelei did the detail work. Our major stipulation was that she stay within budget."

"Look at all the kids," Gina sounded awed. "Didn't anyone start their families young or are these their grandchildren? My two are in their teens, some of these still wear diapers."

Beth noticed Gina staring at a woman hosting a table filled with five spaghetti-slurping boys. The woman was massive with yet another offspring.

"Harriet started her family late and still hasn't quit. She's due in a month."

"She looks blissful," Trista pointed out. "Such an active family must keep her young and fulfilled."

Beth wondered if the tinge of sadness she heard in Trista's tone betrayed sorrow at not having children. Beth occasionally regretted her own childless state. Even if she married Mike—no, when she married him—that wouldn't change because he shared her reluctance to bring children into a crazy world.

Harvey was motioning at them from across the

room. When she waved, he indicated the vacant chairs at his table.

Gina turned her head slightly. "Who is that?"

"Harvey McIntosh."

Gina squinted in his direction. "Of course it is. I didn't recognize him." She waved enthusiastically as she led the group toward him. "You have weathered the years with little outward damage, though I hear you took up a disreputable profession," she said, pulling out the chair next to him.

"We can't all be globetrotting computer software executives. Though I have several patients who are."

"Are you implying something?"

"Only that you chose a stressful lifestyle."

Gina glared at him.

Beth gazed around the room. She darted a look toward the doorway.

Harvey covered her hand with his. "Wade is partying with the football team."

"How thoughtful of him," Jasmine said. "It's like I tell my girls—the ones I counsel—they can't paint their boyfriends as vindictive, nasty creatures just because they won't stand by them. Sometimes the boys are too young for parenting responsibilities, but they have other worthwhile qualities."

"Still seeing nothing but the good in people?" Gina asked.

"It's the way I choose to live," Jasmine replied. She plucked the fan of white linen from her wine glass and caressed its decorative folds.

"Gina is a cynic. Ignore her," Trista reached over and squeezed Jasmine's restless fingers. "Tell us about your lovely daughter. Why isn't she with you?"

"Tiffany had other things to do. Not even the promise of shopping in the world's largest mall could keep her from the first major party of the fall."

"Partying versus shopping, that's a killer decision," Gina mused.

"I'm surprised you let her stay home alone. Is her father supervising?" Trista asked.

"Ralph rarely sees her."

"You should insist that he take part in her upbringing."

"He tries, poor dear, but you know he is so very busy with his new family. They are such darling children."

"The girls I teach would have their boyfriends over in a minute. It's tough to trust them at that age," Trista said.

"Well, Tiffany is very responsible. After all, she is nineteen. Besides, Todd, her fellow, is a sweetheart."

"Nineteen. You were an infant when she was born."

"Very nearly. I was the first in our class to get married and have a child. No, I lie. Marlene and Phil Montgomery beat me."

"I still think she should have supervision."

"Trista, believe me, no harm will come of this."

Silence fell over the table. "Who's going to join me at the buffet?" Beth asked.

After they returned to the table, carrying plates

laden with salad, pasta, and warm rolls, the conversation turned to life stories.

Harvey leaned toward them. "Have any of you run into Bob Dillan yet?"

Beth shook her head. The others did as well.

"Take a look to my left—casually. You see the woman in the low cut, turquoise blouse? The tall one with the long blond hair and scarlet lips."

"The man with her isn't Bob. He's shorter than Bob was at birth," Gina said.

"No, not the man. The woman is Bob, now known as Bobbie."

"No way," Gina said, then looked around to see who had caught her loud outburst. "Damn, I—we fooled around in the backseat of my mom's car one hot summer night." She raised her eyebrows and grinned. "Come to think of it, not much happened."

"She does look lovely. What courage it must have taken to come here tonight. It reaffirms my belief that we should never be ashamed to acknowledge who we are," Jasmine said.

"He's been hanging around the lobby half the afternoon, asking everyone to guess who he is," Harvey said.

"What a great sense of humour," Jasmine said.

"He also tells everyone how he worked as a prostitute to finance the parts of the sex change that health care wouldn't cover."

Beth waited for another cheerfully positive rejoinder, but instead Jasmine asked, "Is that Ms. McKay? Hasn't she aged well? She looks younger than some of us."

"Speak for yourself," Gina quipped. "Though her friend is definitely younger than most of us. Is he one of her students, or her son?"

"She introduced him as her companion," Harvey said, wiping the last of the pasta sauce from his plate with a chunk of focaccia.

"Is he old enough to drink?"

"Gina, stop picking at everyone," Trista said from behind the serviette as she blotted her lips. "Your comments are getting as bad as Dawn's."

"If you attended regularly, you would know gossip is the main entertainment at these events."

"I've done my best to keep in touch with everyone and don't feel it necessary to snipe at them," Jasmine said. "I truly believe a person's childhood friends will stand by one, no matter what. Hollis likes that I keep harmonious connections with people from my past and he agrees that it is important to accept people as they are."

"Holding tight to the past is a waste. It's over and done with and should stay that way," Trista said, crumpling her serviette and tossing it over the remainder of her spinach ravioli.

Beth looked at her, surprised by the venom in her tone. "Well, speaking as someone who has missed every reunion prior to this one, I say reconnecting isn't so bad."

"Not even when dark things crawl out from under rocks?" Trista asked.

"I'll cope with Wade in my own way," Beth said.

"That's not what I meant. What would you do if

someone threatened to expose you as a fraud?"

"What's wrong, Trista? Is it those phone calls? Is someone threatening you? We can call the police. They'll trace the calls and stop the harassment."

"I was just hypothesizing," Trista said. "Really, don't worry. It's nothing. No one is harassing me."

"What calls?" Harvey demanded.

"Just one of my students." A lull fell over the conversation.

"The blonde with the choppy hair, wearing the purple tuxedo, she looks familiar but I can't give her a name." Jasmine pointed to a table near the door.

"Janice Tyler. She's a bigwig in telecommunications. Her date is that cute woman in the glittery slip of a dress."

"What aren't you telling us?" Gina asked, as she motioned for the waiter to refill her wineglass.

"I swear that's all I know."

"Didn't anyone in our group just get married and stay that way?"

"Sure, a few, but what's the fun in talking about them?" Harvey laughed at Trista's shocked expression.

"Did you know Dawn won the lottery just after our last reunion?" Harvey asked.

"She's working at a job she hates," Beth said. "She couldn't have won much."

"She had to share with three others, but ended up with nearly half a million."

"If she invested properly, she'll have a nice nest egg to retire on."

"Except she met Lionel and decided to buy a new version of herself and a new husband. Then her ex fought for a share. Claimed the divorce wasn't final when she bought the ticket. The court sided with her, then he went after custody of their son. That fight got dirty and she lost it. She's appealing, but the rumour is she won't get him back. The court costs are eating up the rest of her winnings."

The remainder of the meal passed as a series of biographies. Harvey seemed to know everything about everyone. However, Beth noted he edited his versions, omitting some of the sordid truths and tempering each story with humour.

As the dessert plates were cleared and the final cups of coffee emptied, families hustled out of the room to enjoy the mall's many diversions.

All Beth wanted was an early night so that she would be ready to tackle Saturday's itinerary, which included the organizing committee meeting, breakfast with Harvey, shopping with her friends, another stint at the registration table, and finally, the actual reunion banquet and dance. Sunday would be peaceful, with only the swim party and picnic beside the wave pool.

Trista and Gina were both flying out Monday morning. Jasmine would start her drive home then too. Beth already felt lonesome. Instead of feeling sorry for herself, she recalled her duties and invited everyone to join her in the hotel lounge.

On the way, she checked the desk for messages, but there were none.

CHAPTER ELEVEN

The group in the lounge expanded and contracted all evening as parents dropped off their kids at one of the movie megaplexes or games emporiums and joined Beth's group for a couple of hours. Some of the sports guys hung around for a few minutes, but they were all gathering at a nightclub where the action was faster and the clientele younger.

Harriet, painfully pregnant, waddled in on the arm of her husband, a handsome fellow with love handles, who seemed determined to fulfil her every wish. They stayed long enough for one soda, then pleaded an impending day of shopping and Galaxyland fever with their sons, and trudged out of the room to relieve their babysitter. Beth watched them walk away, holding hands.

"Do I detect a little jealousy?" Gina asked, nodding toward the retreating couple.

"How do you guarantee that kind of happiness?"

"You don't," Jasmine chimed in. "Though since I've met Hollis, I think I've found it at last."

"Like you did with the other three?" Gina asked.

"Hollis accepts me for who I am, even while he helps me grow."

"He's a politician, right?"

"Yes, Gina, he is one of the devil's spawn, a city councillor."

"It's unfortunate he couldn't attend," Beth said,

hoping to head off any discussion of taste in men or the ethics of politicians.

Jasmine shrugged. "He had a totally unbreakable, long-standing prior commitment."

"So you think he's the man who will make you happy forever?"

"Yes. In fact, I think I'll go call him. It's late anyway and I've had a hellish day. I had to get the boyfriend of one of my girls out of detention—they're planning a birthday party for the baby and he wanted to be there. Then I spent the rest of the morning in court and barely managed to get on the road by noon. I'm beat. Are we still on for shopping tomorrow?" Jasmine asked, as she gathered her purse and pushed in her chair.

"Noon, in the lobby," Beth said, wondering if Mike was the man who would bring her lasting joy.

Carl Lauder leaned toward them, his basketball belly pushing at his shirt. "Is she for real?" he asked as Jasmine left the room. "Her guy probably ran off, throwing phony prior commitments behind him like raw meat to a pack of dogs."

During the time they'd spent as committee members, Beth had learned to tolerate Carl's crude humour, but she didn't appreciate him criticizing her friend. "She's accepting his reason, why don't you?"

"Maybe she's spouting the life is wonderful line as the floor slips out from under her."

"Jasmine always has seen the best in any person or situation."

"Yeah, she sees the golden nugget all right.

Sometimes she even rips it right out of someone's grip."

"Look, she's my friend," Beth said, glaring at him. "Don't run her down."

Carl snorted. "I used to think she was a saint too. Then a buddy's kid got into a shitload of trouble. My bud asked me to put in a word for the kid, figuring I knew people because I worked in the criminal justice system. Jasmine was assessing kids then, making sentencing recommendations. I approached her, figured it was a slam-dunk, 'cause of old times, you know."

Beth didn't know. She'd never heard of any connection between Carl and Jasmine, though his name had been linked to Dawn's for a while.

"When I explained the trouble, she acts all concerned about the kid getting a fair deal, says every kid deserves a second chance, can't see any reason he should be hammered by the system.

"I kept from puking at her optimistic crap, 'cause I'd promised the kid's father I'd help. 'Course, I don't disillusion her with the fact the kid is a little shit. I left the file with her, figuring his release is dead certain. What happens? She gives the kid a piss-poor evaluation and recommends time in detention.

"I go back to her and ask why she made me look like a fool. Oh well, she says, the kid's already a hardened criminal and she won't give him a chance to hurt anyone else."

Carl paused and Beth jumped to Jasmine's defence. "Sometimes not even friendly intervention can divert justice."

"You mean she acted in good conscience? Yeah, I almost bought that line, except when I tell the kid's parents the kid's screwed 'cause Jasmine reneged, my bud's wife clutches her chest like she's having a heart attack and says why didn't I tell her I was talking to Jasmine. When they were kids, she was part of a group who tormented Jasmine a lot."

"You think Jasmine waited a lifetime to get revenge for a school yard squabble? She probably forgot about it ten minutes later."

Carl swallowed the remainder of his beer. "All I know is that when I left her office she was ready to give the kid a break, but two weeks later he's thrown into the system."

He slammed his glass down on the table. "I'm off to find the gang and hunt up some real action."

His story hung over the table like smoke over a campground. Beth tried to think of something to counter his accusations as she watched him glad-hand his way out of the room.

"What a pig," Gina said, breaking into the silence. "Can you imagine Jasmine being intentionally cruel? She's always going on about how kids just need a break. How just one person can turn a kid's life around. I'm glad she has some principles and doesn't let every thug with connections off."

Dawn Richards was table-hopping close enough to hear Gina's comment and marched in their direction. "Not that you have any bias when it comes to Carl, do you Gina?" Her charm bracelet jangled in time with her pointing finger.

"Not a bit. My opinion of his tiny brain, male chauvinistic tendencies, and crude personality are all based on observation and contemplation."

Dawn ignored Gina's retort and turned to Beth. "You weren't at the reunion we had just after Carl was designated scapegoat and forced to resign from the Mounties. Jasmine and Gina were together when they met him at the reunion dinner. Gina looked at him like he was spit on the ground, then turned away. Poor Carl just slithered out of the room. He didn't know Jasmine told us the entire scandal was a set-up. Gina said she was naive and he was a loser who would end his misery with a bullet. It shows you that even Miss Perfect Gina can be wrong. He works as a consultant for a security company."

Gina yawned, patting her lips with her fingers. "And you think he would have been nicer, if he knew Jasmine defended him?"

"We'll never know will we?" Dawn took a sip of water from the bottle she was carrying, then peered at her watch. "Nine thirty meeting tomorrow morning, Beth." She turned toward Gina. "I think I'll go home to my husband. Who do you have to keep you warm at night, Gina, or does any male body do?"

"Bitch," Gina muttered as Dawn retreated.

"Do all reunions take this tone?" Beth asked.

"Hell no. This one is turning into a real brawl." Gina sipped her scotch. "I hope you noted that I didn't retaliate with a comment about her nose job or even inquire about the health of her loving husband's latest girlfriend. I must be mellowing."

"Girlfriend? They've been married less than a year."

"He had a reputation as a stud before he met her, and it hasn't slackened since."

"She did say men couldn't be trusted."

Gina's expression turned dreamy. She sipped her drink, then licked her lips. "Lionel's a rat."

CHAPTER TWELVE

It was shortly after two AM when Beth unlocked the door of her hotel room and turned on the television.

She had left a group in the lounge where they would probably remain until the staff shooed them out. She had pleaded her early meeting and claimed the need to rest, a transparent excuse to escape the sniping that never seemed to end.

She changed into a nightgown, but instead of falling into bed and giving in to exhaustion, she navigated a newly arrived box of reunion records to stare out the window at a slice of the mall's gigantic parking lot. She had found bits and pieces of her classmates in the people she'd encountered that day, but most had changed beyond recognition. She shared a history and a few memories with these strangers, but they had grown so bitter. Was this year unusual? Had the stress generated by Wade's appearance made people edgy?

After Jasmine's retreat and Dawn's vicious outburst, Beth had asked Gina if she felt Jasmine truly had forgiven Wade.

Gina finished her drink and in a practised move motioned for another. "It would take a saint to do that, but with all that rhetoric about accepting people naked and ugly, she'd be a hypocrite if she hadn't. So what's your opinion, hypocrite or saint?"

Beth had been unable to answer. She knew Jasmine

habitually used her Pollyanna attitude to deal with life's speed bumps. Sometimes her infernal habit of seeing only the good in people and situations grated. Still, Beth was glad Wade was staying far away.

"When you met Wade in Bali, had he already heard about the reunion?"

"Said he'd written the bunch of us off. Said he'd made a religion out of avoiding all childhood buddies."

"Then why is he here?"

Gina ran her tongue across her bottom lip and lowered her voice into a seductive purr. "Because I asked him very nicely."

"Quit acting like a slut."

"I beg your pardon!"

"That was uncalled for," Beth admitted, "but you do play the part rather endlessly. Just be straight for once and tell me why he decided to attend."

After a tense moment when Gina seemed to debate walking away, she said, "At first he laughed at me. Said he wouldn't come back for more money than he had stashed in his tax-sheltered offshore accounts. Which, by the way, I doubt was much."

"Why?"

Gina studied her nails, then looked toward Beth with a wry grin. "Just feminine intuition, added to a lot of rumours. He was never the type that money stuck to."

"How long were you in Bali?"

Her fingers flicked through the air as she brushed away the question. "Irrelevant. I talked to people. He gambled."

"And lost?"

"Consistently."

"He spent a lot of money to get here."

"Maybe the gambling is better here."

Gina paused long enough for Beth to become convinced she would not, or could not tell her more, then she sighed. "You had a lot to do with his decision.

"I showed him some pictures from the last reunion. He laughed at his teammates, said they'd gotten old. Then he asked if I had a picture of you. I hesitated on that one, because you haven't gotten old, but eventually I showed him that group picture we took in Mexico. That time with Jasmine and Tiffany.

"That got his attention. Face it girl, he still has a thing for you."

Beth felt uncomfortable and changed the topic. However, the worst thing about the evening came when she phoned Mike and a recorded voice said he was unavailable. Was he still angry, or were events happening so quickly that he didn't want to be interrupted?

She rested her back against the headboard and picked up Mike's picture. His muscle shirt revealed broad shoulders and a deep tan. Bleached hair flecked his bare legs. During that hiking weekend, she had become convinced they belonged together.

Unable to relax, she flicked television channels until she found a black and white movie. Restless, Beth killed the movie and rolled off the bed. Jasmine's room was two doors down the hall. She slipped on a housecoat and out of her room, hoping Jasmine was also awake.

Though she heard the murmur of voices, there was no response to her timid knock. Beth listened closely and realized that the voices came from the same television movie she'd been watching. Jasmine must have used it as a sleep-inducing device.

Beth returned to her room. The bed looked big and cold. She wanted Mike to share it with her. She regretted giving in to her crazy idea of leaving her laptop at home. When she was home and couldn't sleep, she worked.

Beth slipped into jeans and a sweatshirt, grabbed her coat and purse. At this time of night, it was an easy twenty minute drive to her house. She would go home, play with her cats, and check her e-mail. She might even manage a few hours of sleep.

She took the stairs leading to the second floor exit and the parking lot. Wade stood near the door, watching her approach. Beth almost turned and fled. Instead she stiffened her spine and walked toward him.

"Bored already?" he asked, as he crossed his arms and leaned against the door.

"What are you doing here?" Beth asked.

"Waiting for destiny, in the form of you. You always were a night hawk."

He stepped toward her and grabbed her by the shoulders. Beth pushed him away, but he held tight, lowering his lips until they touched hers.

"You know you want me. You always did."

His breath smelled of alcohol.

"You're drunk."

"Still a nag, but I don't care. I came to settle old business and I'm going to do just that."

"Let go," Beth said, twisting to escape, but he was stronger than her.

"Tell me that you love me and always have," he insisted.

Beth broke his grip with an upward swing of her forearms and moved into a defensive stance. He stepped backward.

"Shit, what was that for?"

"Get out of my way."

His expression changed from smugness to resolve as he took a half step forward.

CHAPTER THIRTEEN

Beth threw on jeans and a sweater. She had overslept by twenty minutes and would have to drive like a maniac to get to her meeting on time.

The clouds were low and heavy over Canada Place as she swung around the 98th Avenue traffic circle. A couple of inches of snow had fallen during the night, not enough to make the roads a problem unless it kept up all day. She crossed the North Saskatchewan River at the James MacDonald Bridge. An unprepared driver spun his wheels as he tried to manoeuvre the icy hills leading to the Legislative Building.

Beth turned onto River Road. A few joggers ran along the pedestrian path bordering the river. Slowing to the suggested speed limit, she negotiated the snake-like road. The trees covering the steep hills on either side of the ravine stood out against the white ground.

A stalled car blocked one lane of 107th Street, slowing traffic slightly. The rest of her route ran through a tree-lined residential area until she reached 156th Street when the traffic increased and divided into an octopus of roadways. She drove past several small malls before reaching the 87th Avenue entrance of West Edmonton Mall, where she swept into a parking stall close to the hotel entrance and hurried to the elevators.

Nine-twenty. She had neglected to ask for an early tidy of the room, but if no one had arrived early, she would have time to straighten the bed and close her suitcase before the others arrived. She opened the door, hoping she wouldn't find Carl pawing through her belongings or Dawn scowling at her absence, but the room was dark and silent.

Three steps inside, Beth stopped. The place smelled of vomit. Someone was lying on her bed. Switching on the light, she saw Wade. He was naked except for a purple blanket draped across his middle and something tied around his neck. Her black dress. The scratch marks she had left on his hand were dotted with congealed blood.

She had to get him out of the room before the others arrived. It would be hard enough to explain the scratch marks, but in this context any explanation would feed the gossips.

He hadn't moved when she flipped on the light. She called his name. He didn't stir.

She nudged his shoulder. It was cold and hard.

She backed away, then opened the hall door.

"Watch out, Beth," Harvey said, steadying her as she staggered into him.

"Wade's dead." She pointed to the room.

Harvey released her and stepped inside. He was gone for only seconds and when he returned he was talking on his cellphone.

The elevator doors opened and Dawn strode down the hall toward them. "Sorry I'm late. What are you doing here, Harvey? Is something going on?"

"Wait with Beth," Harvey said, then taking the

keycard from Beth's hand, retreated inside the room and closed the door.

"What was that all about?" Dawn demanded.

"Why are we meeting in the hall?" Carl asked, as he exited the stairwell.

"Something weird is going on," Dawn motioned toward Beth's room.

Beth sagged against the wall as Lorelei, followed by two security guards, hustled into view. "Beth come with me. Harvey wants you to wait for the police somewhere quiet."

"Police?" Carl demanded. "Why? Did someone die or something?"

"Wade," Beth said as she let herself be led away.

Half an hour later, Evan Collins walked into the tiny office where Beth waited sipping coffee. Evan was a homicide detective, and Mike's partner. Though still in his early thirties, his thick body and thinning hair made him look older. His tight lips and brief nod made her uncomfortable.

She extended her hand. "Evan, thank god you're here. I don't know what happened to him."

Evan placed a tape recorder on the desk between them. "Do you mind?" He indicated the machine. When she shook her head, he switched it on and recited the basics necessary to ensure the tape's future worth as evidence.

"You are registered as occupying the room where the deceased, Wade Hamelin, died. Is that correct?"

"I didn't spend the night here. I drove home. I have

no idea why Wade was there. What happened to him? Was it a heart attack?"

"That's the ME's call. I'll talk to the people who knew him best. Maybe he had some medical problem."

Beth shifted in her chair. The adrenaline rush that had propelled her through the last hour was draining fast and weakness was threatening to overwhelm her.

"I knew something was going to happen. Do we call off the reunion—we can't go on like nothing is wrong."

"That's just what you should do, at least until we decide cause of death. But to get back to you, when did you last see the deceased?"

"He spoke to me as I was leaving, sometime around two-thirty."

"Can you prove when you left?"

"There will be a record of when I turned my security system off, and my computer will show when I accessed it. When did he die?"

"That's also up to the ME, but several hours ago."

"I got home around three and left again about nine this morning. If he died between those hours, I guess I could prove I was home."

"Or that your security system was turned off around three. And you turned it back on when you left this morning. Did you turn it on?"

"I don't know. I was late. I might have forgotten."

"We'll check. Did the deceased have a key to your room?"

"No."

"So you invited him inside?"

"No."

"The garment that was wrapped around his neck—is it yours?

"Yes. It's the dress I wore last evening. He wasn't strangled was he?"

"That's for the . . ."

"ME to decide, I know. He had his own room, why did he break into mine?"

"Was he a friend?"

"No, just someone I went to high school with."

Evan studied the cover of his notepad for an uncomfortable moment, then peered up at her and asked, "You have no idea what he was doing in your room?" He waited a beat, then added, "I'm here to investigate his death, not judge your personal life."

He thought—damn. Beth felt a blush spread across her face. Wade had died in her bed, naked. Everyone would be jumping to the conclusion that sex was involved. Who would believe her protests?

"Anything you tell me could help." He waited a few seconds then asked, "Did he use drugs?"

"I don't think so. You think it was an overdose?"

"Did he seem disoriented when you saw him last night?"

"I just saw him for a minute. I think he spent most of the evening with the guys from the football team," Beth explained, but the judgemental look on Evan's face told her she would have to do better. "We weren't friends."

"You're certain you didn't invite him to your room?"

"Don't even think that."

"I heard you used to date."

"A million years ago. We haven't spoken in twenty years."

"Sometimes reunions re-ignite embers."

"Believe me Evan, that wouldn't be the case here even if Mike wasn't in the picture."

"I believe you, Beth. Just stay available. I'll ask the ME to perform a rush autopsy. Lots of out-of-province visitors, so I want this cleared up fast."

Evan clicked off the recorder and flipped his notebook closed. "Don't worry Beth," he said, smiling for the first time. "We'll figure this out, though the black dress necktie is a strange accessory. You'll have an interesting story to tell Mike. How's his father doing?"

Beth appreciated Evan's reassuring words. "I've been trying to reach him, but his phone is turned off."

"Well keep trying, he's probably in the hospital and can't use it. I'm sure he'll call this morning. And don't worry about our investigation—we will do our best to avoid spoiling the fun. Unless we establish foul play, our inquiries will be routine."

"You think someone hurt him?"

"Let's wait until all the evidence is in."

"I forgot to ask how Debra is doing."

Evan's smile seemed ragged. "She's ready to have this baby now, but it's not due for another month. It didn't seem so long with Kenny, but this one has given her trouble from the beginning."

"But she's okay? No major problems?"

"Nothing unusual."

Beth nodded, then fled from the office, into a wall of speculative glances. She grabbed at the high back of a nearby chair as a wave of dizziness swept over her. She shouldn't have rushed from home without eating.

Dawn used her clipboard to push through the crowd. "Do they think Wade was murdered?"

Trust Dawn to anticipate a tragedy. Best stop her speculation before it caused anyone harm. "Murdered? Don't be ridiculous. It was a heart attack or maybe a drug overdose."

Dawn's bottom lip protruded in a pout; she shot a quick look over her shoulder seeking anyone who had heard Beth's rebuke. "Where were you last night? You were supposed to be here, the committee expected you to be here."

"I was restless, so I went home to get some sleep. The committee has to decide what we're going to do."

"About what?"

"We can't ignore his death."

"We have to go on as planned." Dawn looked at the crowd. "It's what people want—what they expect. Why are you being a hypocrite?"

"I found him."

"Okay, so it was a shock, but don't pretend you're grieving. You're probably happy he's dead."

Beth glared at her. It wasn't true.

She left Dawn and made her way through the crowd, trying to gauge how people felt about Wade's death and about continuing with the reunion. All expressed concern and uncertainty, but as several pointed out, they were here, arrangements were made, life had to go on.

Besides, the police wanted to talk to everyone.

Beth stood near the buffet fielding questions and comments. She nibbled on a melon slice and drank coffee. When Carl Lauder appeared, it took only a polite question to start him talking about the night before. After all, who better to watch Wade than an old rival?

"Mostly he was drinking, though he said he had a late date with an old flame." Carl smirked at her. "I'd never have guessed an ice maiden like you could induce heart failure."

Beth felt her hands form into fists. Carl had been a creep in high school and age had only aggravated the trait. A flowery scent flowed around her as a look of disdain settled over Carl's features.

"Go home to your wife and take your dirty little fantasies with you, Carl."

Beth turned toward the voice, ready to berate the speaker for interrupting her impending tirade. Instead, she blinked in surprise, then felt her lips stretch into a smile. The speaker was Bobbie Dillan wearing a floral print skirt and bulky beige sweater.

"I can defend myself, Bobbie," Beth said in a tone far milder than the one she had planned to use.

"I'm amazed that even a creep like you would choose to be a woman," Carl said, turning on his heel and stalking toward the doorway.

Bobbie filled a plate with fruit and muffins. She

handed it to her companion who hovered near her elbow. While pouring them coffee, she said, "Carl always did start talking before thinking. You want to talk into a friendly ear, remember that I'm around."

Without waiting for Beth's response, she followed her friend toward a table, leaving Beth full of adrenaline and aching to work it off.

Gina sauntered to the breakfast buffet, stared at the fresh fruit platter, then turned toward the tray of muffins and croissants. She was dressed for a day of marathon shopping in her designer walking shoes, with a bag no larger than a credit card slung over her shoulder.

"I can't decide whether to be decadent or healthy."

"If my day so far is any indication, you should stock up on calories. Has Evan interviewed you yet?" Beth asked.

Gina fixed her gaze on the buffet. The tongs wavered as they passed over various plates of decoratively arranged food. She shrugged, then glared at Beth. "Some uniformed behemoth pounded on my door, demanding to know what I'd seen and heard in the middle of the night. I told him the twisted moral standards of my fellow attendees weren't my concern."

Gina transferred a croissant to her plate, placed it on the tray beside her black coffee, snagged two pats of butter and a container of grape jelly, then turned toward an empty table. "I don't blame you. I'd have hauled Wade into my room, given the opportunity. You just got to him first."

"I didn't get to him at all. I don't know why he was in my room."

"From what I heard, he was there for fun and games."

"That's a nasty lie."

"You're facing a long stretch of marital monogamy. What better reason to party while you can?"

A shriek of anger rose in Beth's throat. She swallowed hard. Gina was upset. Once she found out why Wade had broken into her room, and why he had died in that bizarre pose, life would return to normal.

"What time did you leave the lounge?" Beth demanded.

"Around three. I hung around the lobby for a few minutes, hoping Wade would appear. We hadn't arranged anything specific because he'd said earlier that he had plans. I thought he meant drinking with the guys, but I guess you knew different. When he didn't show, I left Trista and Harvey mentally pawing each other and went upstairs."

She tore a tiny chunk from the croissant, smeared it with butter, then popped it into her mouth.

"As I left the elevator," she stared at Beth, then looked down, "I saw Wade go into your room." She further mutilated the pastry. "I've been unusually slow getting the message, but then you're a better actress than I gave you credit for."

Much of what Gina said didn't make sense, but Beth latched onto the fact that she had seen Wade. "How did he get inside?"

"You dragged him in."

"Not me. I left the hotel around two-thirty."

Gina's pencil thin eyebrows shot skyward and a tinge of doubt shaded her expression. "Well, I saw a feminine arm grab him and he stumbled forward like an eager puppy."

"Would you recognize the woman?"

"Just saw the arm."

"You told Evan?"

"That cute detective?" Gina shook her head. "Give me more points for discretion than that. I don't tell cops who I see going into my friends' hotel rooms."

Gina had to tell Evan, but what if he thought it was her? Her credibility and her story of going home would be further discounted as a creative alibi.

"What time, exactly, did you see Wade?"

Gina popped the final piece of pastry into her mouth and licked her fingertips clean. She inspected her long nails for flaws, then picked up her coffee mug.

"Exactly—I don't know. Ask Harvey or Trista if they noticed when I left. You know, I think something is brewing between those two."

"Did anything stand out about the person you saw letting him into my room? Maybe the colour of dress was she wearing? Was she tall or short?"

Gina closed her eyes. When she opened them again, she placed her hands on the edge of the table and stood.

"Yesterday was a bitch with that long flight and the time change. I took my contacts out because they were giving me a headache. Maybe I even drank a bit too much. Plus, I admit it, I was feeling a tad nervous that you might be glad to see Wade."

Beth grabbed her hand. "It wasn't me. Honest Gina, it wasn't me."

Gina tilted her head and studied Beth. Something clicked in her expression and the doubt Beth had seen earlier wavered.

"Well, maybe it wasn't. I didn't see a lot of detail. But the man was Wade. I should tell the cops I saw him, right?"

"You have to."

"Well, I want to get a couple of things done first. Damned if I'm hanging around here just to talk to them. Are we still on for shopping?"

Beth nodded. Life must go on—but her thoughts weren't on shopping.

As Gina glided through the pedway leading to the mall, Beth's cellphone chimed.

CHAPTER FOURTEEN

On his way to the cafeteria for more coffee, Mike stepped outside the hospital's main entrance and dialed Beth. She sounded distracted even though her first question was about his father's condition. Her delight that he was going to recover was tempered when Mike added that no one knew to what extent.

Mike apologized for pressuring her to go to Saskatchewan, then, as penance, added, "Look, stay in Edmonton, enjoy your friends. There's nothing to do here but wait and watch anyway."

"Are you certain? I could come, really."

Something in her voice sounded strange, and it wasn't just her eagerness to be at his side. "What's wrong?"

"Are you talking to Evan today?"

"Has something happened?"

"We've had a bit of excitement. One of the guys died during the night. Probably a heart attack."

"Was his heart problem known? Has the ME signed off on it?"

"Apparently they have to do an autopsy. Evan is questioning everyone who saw him last night."

"That sounds like more than a natural death inquiry. What else is going on?"

Beth hesitated, then said, "I found him in my room."

Mike waited for her to continue speaking as various

scenarios played havoc with his emotions.

"I went home last night because I couldn't sleep. I don't know what he was doing in there."

Keeping his voice level was a challenge, but Mike knew he could accept her explanation. "I'll talk to Evan and find out what's going on."

"You have to concentrate on your dad. You can't worry about what's going on here."

Beth's reassurance sounded falsely brave.

"I'll make time." He cringed at the way his words snapped through the receiver, but she responded with an urgent recital of a witness statement and a plea for advice.

"Let me talk to Evan before you start panicking. Make sure your friend talks to him too. If the cause of death is natural, her information could lead to a witness. If there are other considerations—well, I'll talk to Evan about that. Do you want me to come back?"

He wanted her to say she needed his shoulder to lean on and his arms around her for comfort.

"Your family needs you. I'm sure things will calm down long before you can get here. I'll probably go home tonight anyway—I certainly won't sleep in that room."

He wanted her to take the next plane to be with him, even though it was impractical.

CHAPTER FIFTEEN

Harvey watched Beth return her phone to her pocket and slump into a chair. She'd better hear the worst from him.

He saw welcome in Beth's eyes when she looked up. She couldn't be the cause of Wade's death, especially if he had died in the way Harvey suspected. He rested his hand on her shoulder, then sat in the chair next to her.

"I guess our breakfast will have to wait until tomorrow. Have you eaten anything?"

"Not really hungry. Thank you for taking over and calling the police. When I first saw him lying there, all I could think about was getting him out of my room before someone started rumours. Until I touched him, I thought he was passed out. Was it a heart attack? Why were you there anyway? We weren't meeting until ten-thirty."

"I was on my way for an early jog around the mall."

Harvey closed his eyes and the scene in Beth's room sprang into view. That black fabric around Wade's neck, a blanket across his waist. His legs motionless. His tanned chest unmoving. His eyes staring. Bloody foam around his mouth. Vomit staining the carpet.

The scene had reminded him of Karen, so he'd had to pass his suspicions along to the medical people. When he opened his eyes, Beth was staring at him.

"I saw a similar death a couple of years ago," he said, debating how to continue. "It was a drug overdose."

She placed her hand over his. "Evan said something about drugs. What kind of drug?"

"Have you heard of date rape drugs?"

"I've helped high school students research the topic. They render people compliant. There are some well-documented cases of women experiencing flashbacks to a rape that took place days before, but people don't die from them."

"There's more than one kind. If I'm right, the drug Wade took is called Gamma Hydroxy Butyrate or GHB. In small quantities, it has lots of uses. It relaxes your inhibitions and increases your sex drive. It's even used to help people sleep. Larger doses can cause vomiting and unconsciousness. People who take it can seem intoxicated or become extremely violent or indiscriminately sexual.

"In large doses it can depress breathing, though it is usually a combination of vomiting and unconsciousness that leads to death. One of my patients died that way. I had to identify her body."

For months, he had worked to help Karen overcome the trauma of being raped, only to fail dismally when she became addicted to the same drug that had been used on her. He had warned her of its unpredictability, had told her that every time she used it she risked an overdose.

He looked into Beth's eyes. "The stuff is advertised

on-line as a cure-all for inhibitions and most times it's used with no ill effects. All sorts of people use it, so if you want to talk about last night, you won't shock me and absolutely anything you tell me will remain confidential."

The scornful expression on her face told Harvey he had guessed wrong. At least about Beth's involvement, but who could blame him for jumping to that conclusion? He had seen other couples reunite at reunions and conferences. Was the idea of them using the drug to calm their guilt and nervousness so strange?

Beth fiddled with the flatware on her empty plate. "I was not with Wade. I was at home. But, with even my friends doubting me, I guess I'll have trouble proving it."

"I should have known better, but it's been so long since we've talked. Look, I'll help any way I can."

Beth's glare slowly fizzled and was replaced by her natural optimism. "Do you remember what time Gina left you last night?"

"Trista and I talked for a while after she went upstairs. I got to my room sometime after three. I can't be more exact than that."

"I'm going for walk," Beth said. "In fact I'm going to hit the gym. I do my best thinking when I'm sweating."

CHAPTER SIXTEEN

"Beth," Lorelei called as Beth crossed the lobby. "Was he a good friend? It's so awful. The police said you can't use your room until they've finished investigating."

"I don't want to go back there anyway."

"Right, so I looked for another room, but we're absolutely full. You aren't the squeamish type, are you? I can juggle the records and give you the dead guy's room. It's a theme room on another floor, but at least you'll have somewhere to crash."

Beth waited for Lorelei to wind down. Wade's room? He hadn't been in it long, but maybe his belongings could tell her why he'd died—and especially why he'd died in her room.

"Are the police finished with it?"

"They said they'd notify us when housekeeping can clean it."

"You'll have my luggage transferred?"

"I'll make the arrangements."

The girl's sympathetic tone crystallized the morning's trauma in a way that all the flustered worrying, gossip, and recriminations hadn't. Beth felt tears well in her eyes and brushed them away. She would not break down in the middle of the lobby with half of her old classmates looking on.

Lorelei plunged her hands into her pockets and

looked away. "I want to go over a couple of last-minute details about tomorrow's pool party. I'm away for the rest of today, but the catering staff needs final input on the set up. Can we meet in the morning? Say ten-thirty?"

Beth nodded, then asked, "Would it be out of line to ask you to do the paperwork on the room change and give me the key now?"

Lorelei's pained expression had her adding, "It would eliminate complicated explanations."

"I suppose it will be all right. But don't use it until housekeeping's finished."

"Of course," Beth said.

Lorelei changed the computer records and after handing over the new key card, disappeared into her office. Beth hurried to the elevators.

Wade's room was on the eighth floor. The hallway had a dotted white line running down the middle. Trust Wade to choose to sleep in the back of a pickup truck!

She opened the door to his room slowly, composing a plausible excuse for any police officer waiting inside. Dim light filtered through a gap in the curtains. She noted the stand of traffic lights first, then the statue of the policeman, whistle to his lips guarding the Jacuzzi. A gas pump added to the room's ambience.

Finally, she let her gaze rest on the room's centrepiece, a bright yellow truck. It dominated the room and she sidled around it, though there was ample space to walk. Even the pictures on the wall featured macho vehicles.

A mattress filled the truck bed. Mike's feet would hang over the end. A mirror covered the ceiling above it. Beth stared at the blinking traffic lights and wondered how to shut them off.

An open suitcase sat on the luggage rack. Two others sat near the wall and a garment bag hung from the coat rack. Too much clothing for a weekend. Beth lifted one of the cases. It was heavy.

She returned to the open case and traced a finger across the top layer of clothing, then lifted a casual shirt and a pair of slacks, uncovering a couple of dress shirts.

Gina's speculation that Wade was job hunting seemed probable. Beth looked toward the other cases. Perhaps he had already landed a new position and this move was permanent?

As she replaced the shirt and slacks, Beth spotted the corner of an envelope protruding from under the dress shirts. She pulled it out and peered inside. Notices about the reunion and bios of the attendees.

Beth looked over her shoulder at the statue of the policeman. Her breathing accelerated. With shaky hands and dry lips, she checked the side compartments. Her breathing sped. Footsteps approached, setting off her internal alarms, until they continued down the hall.

Wet towels on the bathroom floor told her Wade had taken a shower before his evening of carousing. A medicinal scent drifted from his toiletry bag. She checked its jumbled contents for heart medicine. She also searched it for a container of the drug Harvey had mentioned. If he'd brought it through customs, it might be in something common like a film canister or a breath mint container.

A folded sheet of hotel stationery lay beside the phone. With a quick look over her shoulder, she unfolded it. A picture fell face down. Beth studied the word 'Dana' written on the back. Beth flipped it over.

A girl wearing jeans and a T-shirt stared at her. The backdrop was rural, with rolling hills and farm buildings in the distance. The girl's smile seemed posed. She seemed vaguely familiar.

Beth unfolded the sheet of paper. Scribbled on it was "#51 by the Conference Centre, 2:45," with no signature.

That was the entrance where Wade had accosted her. Had he been waiting for someone? The girl in the picture? Perhaps she was staying in the hotel. That would explain Beth's sense of familiarity.

She refolded and replaced the note, then sent a quick look toward the statue of the policeman. When he remained silent, she tipped one of the remaining cases flat on the floor and flipped open its latches.

More clothes, beach clothes. His resumé, three letters of reference, and a picture of him on a beach in the midst of a group of revellers. The second case held more clothes. He must have come back to stay.

Again loud voices slid under the door. Deciding she was pushing her luck, Beth snapped the cases closed and returned them to their place against the wall. She looked around, fearful of having left some sign of her presence. Then she fled to the mall to buy the clothes she needed for her workout.

CHAPTER SEVENTEEN

Mike stood outside the entrance of the rural hospital in Humbolt, Saskatchewan, a small town in the centre of the province. The air smelled fresh, though the sky was grey and heavy with clouds. A crumpled sheet of newspaper skittered around his feet before joining the collection of litter piled against the red brick wall.

A Ford Supercab pulled into a spot between a Sonoma and a Ranger. When the doors opened, five children spilled out. One of the kids, a boy dressed in miniature jeans and a tiny jean jacket, followed the group. He struggled to balance a large potted plant that was taller than he was. His mother fluttered around him, hoping to prevent a disaster.

But disasters were hard to stop. Mike knew his mother needed his support to get through this one, but he didn't know how to comfort her. Damn—life never waited until you were ready.

He looked across the street toward the shopping area where people were going about life as if nothing extraordinary had happened. Tragedy was a personal event, but most of his experience with it came from the investigative side.

He'd feel better if the hospital staff would let him do something other than wait for some sign that all would be well. In his helplessness, he found himself studying the medical staff. When they asked his father to push against their hands, or to squeeze their fingers, Mike caught himself straining, willing his father to make some movement that would meet with their approval.

John and his wife had spent the morning at home, feeding cattle and resting. They had returned only an hour earlier, wanting to relieve his mother's vigil. When she refused to leave his father's bedside, they turned their attention toward him.

At first, he had refused to abandon his mother. Then his father, though drowsy and befuddled, slurred some words that seemed to reinforce their argument.

Mike knew it was time to give in to sleep. He had been at the hospital since arriving in town the previous afternoon, without sleep for more than thirty-six hours.

Still, he had waited to speak to the doctor before leaving. He wanted his dad moved to Saskatoon. The doctor refused permission, arguing that they were using the most modern techniques to minimize damage. But the doctor was a kid, too young to be an expert at anything.

Mike's nurse friend assured him the doctor was in fact a top man who was in town to inspect their new equipment and instruct staff in the latest stroke treatments. His dad, she claimed, was fortunate in his timing. As if anyone suffering a stroke could be considered fortunate. Besides, she promised, the care they gave members of their own community was superior to anything he would receive in an anonymous teaching hospital.

Eventually giving in to their arguments, Mike scrubbed at his face to relieve the drag of fatigue and agreed to leave for a short time.

Mike wished Beth could be with him. He pulled his cellphone from his pocket and punched Evan's number. At least he could find out exactly what was going on.

From the background noise, Mike knew he had caught Evan's son, Kenny, in the midst of a screaming fit. Kenny was nearly three years old and going through a phase that made Mike remember why he didn't want kids.

When he recognized Mike's voice, Evan asked him to hang on until he could get somewhere quiet. The screaming faded, then abruptly died.

"I figured I'd be hearing from you," Evan said.

Mike thought he sounded more tired than usual.

"Debra is feeling lousy. She thinks the baby is coming. With them forecasting a big dump of snow, we don't want to risk waiting, so we're dropping Kenny at her mom's house, then checking in with the doctor."

"That's great. I wish you luck getting that little girl you want." Mike tried to sound enthusiastic. He truly was happy for them because they were a couple that deserved all the good things in the world, but he needed information or he was going to go crazy.

"I'll make this quick," Mike said. "What's going on at West Edmonton Mall? Beth said she found a body in her hotel room. Is it a natural death?"

"Beth's doctor friend alerted the medical technicians to the possibility of a GHB overdose. Sent up flags or we might have waited to perform a routine autopsy."

"The ME is up to speed?"

"I asked for a rush on the blood and told the crime scene people to check for drug paraphernalia."

Mike pulled up his jacket collar to shield his neck from the bite of the cold north wind. "Any tie to Beth, except him being found in her room?"

"Both the victim and the doctor were reunion participants. Beth says she was unable to sleep and went home. She doesn't know how, or why, the man died in her room."

That sounded like Beth—she needed about two hours of sleep to keep going at the frantic pace she considered normal.

"I've learned the dead guy, Wade Hamelin, worked outside of Canada ever since he finished high school. He was Beth's boyfriend back then. From what I've gathered, the doctor was one of her conquests too. It's tough getting much information from her classmates. Makes me wonder why they're so protective of her."

"She never mentioned a Wade Hamelin to me."

"Probably didn't think it was important. They broke up twenty years ago and the consensus is they hadn't met since, until yesterday." Evan told him about the scene in the lounge.

"Beth said she also saw him on her way out of the hotel last night. We haven't found anyone who admitted talking to him after that and we haven't discovered what he was doing in her room. No sign of tampering or forced entry. Too many prints to sort out quickly, but we're eliminating what we can."

"What about the doctor?"

"Dr. Harvey McIntosh, says he's an old friend who was passing her door on his way to the mall. Apparently they were planning to meet for breakfast later on. He's saying nothing more about their friendship, but it's obvious he's willing to play hero for her."

"What's his connection with the dead guy?"

"As far as I can discover, they're just old classmates. Same as everyone else here."

Kenny's screaming suddenly pierced the background hum and Mike heard Debra call for Evan. Mike didn't want to be the cause of their baby being born on the way to the hospital, but he needed the answer to one more question.

"Was he a known user?"

"No one has said so, but we found a glass near the body that's being checked for drug residue. He was drinking with cronies earlier, but no one noticed any of the usual symptoms. He could have brought the stuff with him, might even be an addict who uses low doses to keep a constant buzz going. Add a bit too much alcohol and you have an overdose.

"A woman saw the victim going into Beth's room."

"Beth told me."

"Sorry Mike, but I've got to get going. Babies don't wait."

The line went dead. Mike leaned against the icy brick wall. The air was chilly. He had neglected to throw his winter jacket or his heavy boots into his truck before starting out. He looked across the road and decided to use some of his restless energy restocking his emergency kit for the trip home, as well as buying clothes to last him for the few days he planned to stay.

Who was this old boyfriend? And what about the doctor she was meeting for breakfast? This reunion was supposed to be her chance to meet up with her three best friends from high school. The three friends she had mentioned were women.

Not that he was jealous, but why had she neglected to mention those two men?

CHAPTER EIGHTEEN

Beth walked alongside a geology display that featured a stunning array of crystals. It dominated the branch corridor leading from the second floor of the hotel to the main throughway of the mall. She spotted Trista and Jasmine admiring the replica of the Santa Maria floating in the Pirate Lagoon.

Gina approached from the entrance to Phase IV, passing under the tail of the huge metallic dragon that breathed fire in the lobby of one theatre megaplex.

The mall was filled with the usual Saturday crowd and swollen to exploding with pre-Christmas shoppers. Families pushed strollers. Clusters of teenage girls carried shopping bags advertising exclusive and trendy stores.

Groups of boys jostled each other as they walked side-by-side, daring people to meet them head on. Others checked out the latest gaming software, unaware that other shoppers were entitled to equal browsing rights.

Bored middle-aged men sat outside dress shops. Seniors crowded cafés and sidewalk tables looking for company and gossip.

Some of the earliest risers hugged their friends, fastened jackets, and searched for their gloves as they headed toward the parking lot. At her high school graduation, Gina and one other girl of oriental background, and one boy whose ancestors originated in Africa had represented the world's visible minorities. Looking around the mall now, she saw a snapshot of Edmonton's current cultural mix that included a full spectrum of ethnic groups.

Beth dodged a couple of excited kids and circled an elderly woman driving a motorized cart. She looked through the glass ceiling at the falling snow. The storm had settled in.

After buying shorts and a T-shirt, Beth had sweated off her fatigue and frustration. She showered in the gym, then changed into the jeans, turtleneck, and runners she had thrown on when she rolled out of bed. Her friends wanted to spend a few hours shopping and she certainly wasn't returning to Wade's room until it had been sanitized and her belongings moved in.

Some of the rush she'd felt while rummaging through Wade's belongings lingered. If only she had found something that indicated an underlying heart condition. Or something to substantiate Harvey's drug theory. But finding the cause of death was Evan's job. She would spend time in the company of her friends and try to salvage the rest of the reunion.

Jasmine, clad in jeans and a pink sweater set, greeted her with an enthusiastic smile. Her obvious display of pleasure in light of Wade's death was almost obscene. Gina seemed sheepish. But Trista appeared distracted. Beth wondered if her intrusive student was still phoning.

Beth and her friends watched a tourist-filled submarine slide silently through the lagoon. In the distance, the bridge over the lagoon was crowded with spectators trying to secure the ultimate view of the diving show finale.

Then Beth pointed her friends toward the mall's second floor, which she thought had a quieter and classier atmosphere.

They window shopped their way down the mall, detouring to stare at the swimmers in the Water Park. She recognized several reunion participants on deck chairs, enjoying the warm air while snowflakes melted on contact with the glass ceiling.

They turned away from the pool and Gina spotted the Antique Photo Parlour. She insisted they get a picture and chose a saloon girl look for her costume. Trista picked a sedate schoolmarm dress and Jasmine chose the richness of an upstanding citizen.

Beth chose a mauve gown that was low in the bust and high on the thigh. Mike would appreciate a copy and she would cherish it above any candid shot that might make its way into their reunion's memory book.

As they left the photo shop, Beth spotted the mall's cleaning crew, polishing the miles of brass and glass railings. The water splashing in the fountains on the main floor was audible, but not the roar that drowned the conversations of people walking beside the miniature plant lined ponds and streams.

Gina checked the winter stock in every boutique. Trista searched bargain racks for summer wear. Beth and Jasmine, with no incentive to snap up goods priced in discounted Canadian dollars and free of provincial sales tax, browsed with casual interest.

While waiting outside one store, Beth ran her fingers over the woollen fabric of a suit jacket. "Jasmine," she said, trying to sound casual, "I dropped by your room around two-thirty last night. The television was on, but you didn't answer when I knocked. Did anything wake you up around then?"

Jasmine looked up from the embroidered cardigan she was holding. "I slept like a log, once I fell asleep. Had to take a couple of sleeping pills of course," she added. "It's something I do when I'm in strange surroundings or if I allow something to upset me."

"Why do you think Wade decided to show up at this reunion?"

"Facing us was important for his personal healing. I'm glad I forgave him before he died. It helped me and may have eased his passing."

Beth doubted she would ever forget Wade's behaviour and as for forgiveness, well, it was irrelevant now. As she studied Jasmine's smug expression, a sneaky thought intruded. "When did you see him to forgive him?"

"I forgave him in my heart." Jasmine dropped the sweater and turned to face Beth directly. Her mouth puckered and she narrowed her eyes. "Don't look at me like that. Don't you think I see how you and the others snicker because I find the positive side of things? I deal with kids who have fallen off society's tracks. They run from homes so terrible it's hard to believe the trouble they find on the streets could be worse. If I couldn't see the positive in every situation I would have quit by now, or turned into one of my cynical co-workers."

"I did admire how calmly you reacted when you heard he was here. You were more profoundly affected by Wade's actions than I was, and I froze when I saw him."

Jasmine retrieved another sweater from the bin, looked at it, then folded it, and replaced it before replying. "Life is too short, as the saying goes, to waste as much as a millisecond on hatred."

Trista and Gina strolled out of the store empty-handed. The group continued wandering, eventually stopping above the Ice Palace. A local figure skating class twirled around the huge ice arena.

"So, I guess the reunion committee couldn't arrange for the Oilers to practise here today," Gina said.

"The team is on the road for the next couple of weeks," Beth replied.

Jasmine turned away from the rink and headed toward a coat display at the rear of another store.

Beth followed Trista to the bargain racks and as they examined items, asked, "Do you recall what time Gina left you and Harvey last night?"

"Two-fifty."

"You're sure? The others weren't."

Trista extended her lightly tanned wrist, displaying a turquoise watch face in a tooled silver band. "I'm compulsive about knowing the exact time and always wear one of my watches."

It would have taken Gina less than five minutes to

reach the elevators and ascend to the seventh floor.

The note in Wade's toiletry case had arranged a meeting for 2:45. The woman Gina had seen with Wade must have been the person he was meeting. Wade knew Beth had left the hotel. But why break into her room?

Still, if Gina had seen Wade at 2:50, Beth could prove she had left the hotel by then. It took twenty minutes to drive across town and she had turned off her house alarm around three o'clock.

Trista's cellphone played its tune. She pulled it from her purse and looked at the display. With a violent jabbing motion, she turned the phone off. She stared at it, calming her rapid breathing before looking at Beth. An irked grin twisted her lips. "That student is going to fail just for being a nuisance."

"Do you miss having children of your own?" Beth asked. "I do, sometimes, but I suppose because you're around kids so much, it's not the same for you."

Trista replaced the slacks she had been examining and rummaged further along the rack. "See if you can find this style in black, in a size ten," she said. "Are you regretting not having kids long ago, or trying to decide whether to have them once you're married to Mike?"

"I think Mike is a little upset with me right now. I should be with him, at least until his father is out of danger."

"Men are little more than spoiled children. Always wanting you to be at their right hand. I suppose he's putting pressure on you to breed like a rabbit in the years you have left?"

"Mike would never behave that way."

Beth watched a family group approach. The teenaged daughter was arguing loudly against entering a particular store. Her mother, wearing an impatient scowl, opened her purse and thrust some bills at the girl. Then she pointed to a nearby café and said she would be waiting and the girl could buy whatever she wanted.

Was that how Trista was feeling? Was she ready to strike out because a student had upset her?

After two hours of browsing, Beth led them to the Café Europa for coffee and cheesecake. Once seated around a table, the women rehashed their impressions of former classmates.

Joe Small had turned into a lush in dire need of counselling. Pete Hargrove shouldn't be in charge of greeting teachers he had tormented throughout high school. Janice Tyler's sexual preference wasn't a surprise. Gina compared Bobbie Dillan's new breasts to a work of art.

Everyone agreed Carl Lauder won the contest for the most obnoxious male, though Trista felt Arnie Hancock came a close second. Beth wondered if the football team attracted creeps or encouraged men to turn into them.

"Carl hated Wade," Jasmine said, making the rest of them frown at her harsh judgement.

"Hate is too strong a word. They were rivals, but they did everything together," Beth protested.

"I've seen examples of similar behaviour with my

kids," Jasmine said, as she stared toward the European storefronts lining Europa Boulevard. "It looks like hero worship, but it's really one kid watching his enemy very closely. Carl wanted the popularity Wade enjoyed. He wanted to be the football star and the class Romeo. Wade owned both titles."

"Girls may have fantasized, but Wade was never a Romeo," Beth said.

"Well," Gina said, breaking the thick silence that followed Beth's statement. "He has certainly earned that title lately. He had quite a reputation around that hotel he managed."

"Lonely women on holiday. He probably just got tired of fending them off."

"No. If our encounter was anywhere near typical, he was definitely operating in offensive mode."

Beth stared at Gina, intent on making her clarify or retract her statement. Gina lifted her chin and looked down her sculpted nose.

"I don't know how Harriet manages her five sons," Jasmine said, as she leaned forward and stretched her arms across the table to touch their hands.

The change of topic wasn't subtle, but it worked. Beth relaxed against the high back of her chair and patted her lips with her serviette. "You have to admire Maggie and Phil Montgomery for sticking together for so long. Sometimes it seems everyone I know is divorced."

"Some marriages last, though Maggie Hartwell's habit of hugging everyone in sight is creepy. I don't know how her husband stands it," Gina added.

Harvey, they all agreed, was a busybody, though a nice one. Trista defended him by pointing out that it was his business to delve into people's psyches. Gina countered with the suggestion that he should restrict his delving to patients.

Beth was not surprised when Wade's name resurfaced. Her friends agreed that of the men, Wade had aged best. Gina, with a casual flick of her fingers and a knowing smile, said he had been one of the best lovers she had ever had.

"That week with him was worth the twenty years we waited. How high did you rank him, Beth?"

Jasmine shrank against the back of her chair. Trista wrapped her arms around her bust. They obviously felt as uncomfortable as Beth did with Gina's brash comments.

Gina tilted her head and waited for Beth's answer.

"I don't rank men."

"He must have scored pretty high, since you haven't found a permanent replacement."

"Gina, this is uncalled for," Trista's voice cracked like a whip, cutting the final strands of politeness. Gina glared at her. Jasmine squirmed in her chair.

"I should be getting back," Beth said, trying to divert the animosity she felt building. "I do want to talk to Evan again. He must know more by now."

"Before you run off, tell us about your wedding plans. You've been engaged for ages, you must have things nearly ready to go," Jasmine said, again smoothing the waters.

Beth saw avid curiosity in their faces and felt trapped. "We haven't set a date. It's impossible to set aside time to plan even a small wedding."

"So lasso a Justice of the Peace and do the deed real quick and quiet," Gina suggested.

"Co-ordinating time off for a honeymoon is complicated."

"So delay it."

"I suggested eloping, but Mike wants a big wedding. He said that by the time we invite all his family and mine, we might as well rent a hall and do it up right."

"But you're not into making all those arrangements," Trista said.

"I helped get this reunion together and hated every minute I wasted on menus and decorations."

"My parents did the Justice of the Peace thing," Gina said. "Then they drove to Jasper for a weekend of skiing. They've been married nearly fifty years."

Beth thought of the simplicity of such an act and felt some of the tension in her neck ease. "Too many people would be disappointed."

"As long as neither you nor Mike is in that number, who cares," Gina pointed out as she stood and turned toward the restaurant door. "Well whatever you do, let me know. I still have a few hours of energy left and a whole lot of mall to cover. I saw a statue I liked in one of the art shops. Decided to think about it for a while, but I keep remembering its sinuous lines. It was almost hypnotic. I just might track it down again. Are we still meeting for cocktails at five?"

"I told Harvey we would be in the Fantasy Lounge. He seemed keen on joining us," Trista said.

"Well, we can't disappoint Harvey can we? I should have maxed out a few credit cards by then anyway," Gina said, as she left them.

Jasmine ordered more coffee, saying she wanted to people watch. Trista was returning to the hotel. Beth suggested she contact the school and put a stop to the phone calls. Her sickly smile made Beth wonder who and what was really behind those calls.

CHAPTER NINETEEN

Beth usually avoided the noisy, crowded food fair, but today her drive for fresh baked bread led her into its depths. The howls of flushed and cranky children nearly deterred her, but the yeasty scent of fresh cinnamon buns and the improbable aroma of coffee blending with the salty tang of soy sauce led her on.

Hurrying toward the bakery, Beth spotted Harriet waving, her hand a swaying beacon among the occupants of the crowded area. As Beth reluctantly approached, Harriet cleared away the parcels surrounding her, encouraging Beth to take a seat.

"The guys are in there," she pointed at Galaxyland, the mall's in-house fairgrounds. Colourful structures filled the entranceway of the huge area. Screams of joyful terror nearly overwhelmed the mechanical roar of the rides.

Harriet patted her extended abdomen, her hand coming to a rest on its broad top. "We've been going crazy with early Christmas shopping. This little girl is going to make the season too busy for me to get out much longer."

"You're finally getting a girl?"

"That's what the ultrasound said," Harriet sighed, then rubbed her hand over the bulge. "I would have stopped long ago, but we felt it was important to have a daughter."

"My parents did the same, except with them it was three girls, then a boy."

Harriet rested her elbow on the table and cupped her chin in her hand. Her smile dimmed and her eyelids fought to close. "This isn't how I had my life planned. With a doctorate in biochemistry I was aiming for fame, but ended up with six kids. I should be committed."

Beth mumbled a denial that she didn't believe. In her opinion, anyone with that many kids and no nanny was nuts.

"I know what people think, but I don't understand how you can be happy with no one to care for. In school you were the person we all thought would settle down with a bunch of kids and I was going to be the Nobel Prize-winning scientist. Life sure does laugh at our plans."

Beth remembered her school girl dream of marrying Wade. In her dream, their life was perfect. They went through university together, and then married, and had a daughter and a son. She was a stay-at-home mom until the kids started school. She and Wade grew old together, trusting, watching over and caring for each other.

Wade had destroyed that dream. Seeing how he reacted after the accident had opened her eyes and she knew that her dream was dead, forever. Now she knew marriage was a big enough gamble. Dreams of family were dangerous and best left buried.

"You and Wade seemed so perfect. He went crazy

when you dumped him. When I heard he was coming to the reunion, I thought maybe time had healed your wounds. It would have been so romantic if you had gotten back together."

Beth ignored her wistful fantasies. "How did you know he was coming?"

Harriet placed the palms of her hands on her stomach, protecting her baby from Beth's sharp demand. She scrunched her face in concentration. "I don't recall. There's a lot I don't remember these days. I don't know why being pregnant gives me short-term memory loss, but it's happened every time."

"I wouldn't know," Beth muttered. "You really knew he was coming before yesterday?"

Harriet sucked the last of the milk from her carton and placed the container on the tray.

"Someone probably told me or maybe I read it in an e-mail. I think that may have been it, just his name on a routine update of attendees."

"I got the impression Wade's registration was a last minute thing."

"It could have been," Harriet said as she grasped the edge of the table and pushed to her feet.

"How long have you known?"

"At least a month. Before I ballooned anyway." She turned at the cry of 'Mom' coming from the depths of Galaxyland. "I'm being paged, so I guess rest time is over."

It was no wonder she had felt the spotlight of attention. If everyone knew Wade was attending, they probably thought she knew as well. They must have thought she was there just to reignite their romance.

She was going to strangle Dawn for not warning her.

CHAPTER TWENTY

The committee meeting was nearly pointless since the conversation kept swinging back to Wade's death. Dawn made it plain that she believed Beth was somehow responsible, if only for abandoning her post. What if, she demanded, Wade had gone to Beth's room expecting help and found her gone?

Beth asked her how long Wade's name had been on the list of attendees. Dawn studied the bird of paradise pattern on the carpet. She cleared her throat a few times, then looked back at Beth and unleashed her outrage.

"You received the same lists as everyone else and if you didn't bother reading them, well that's too bad."

Carl snickered and Beth read the dirty thoughts behind his smirk. She wanted to proclaim that she had not caused Wade's heart attack in the throes of passion or in any other way. Fortunately, Gina's sighting was not common knowledge, nor had Harvey spread his drug theory.

She forced them through the agenda as quickly as she could, then suffered through her final shift at the registration desk before going to the lobby, hoping for an update from Evan.

The desk clerk said Evan had been called away. Did she wish to leave a message? Beth squeezed her room card in her left hand as she wrote a note asking him to call. If she could explain the death at the banquet, everyone would relax. If she could discover why Wade had died in her room, she would relax.

Then she fled to the elevator, dreading a return to Wade's room with its awful truck decor. However, the staff had cleared his belongings and she felt no lingering trace of him as she sat in the chair and looked toward the truck bed. This macho haven would have been her last choice of room. Maybe if she spoke to Lorelei, begged for the next available vacancy, she could get out of here. Still, it was a quiet place that gave her a reprieve from prying eyes and curious questions.

She wanted to abandon her duties and flee the hotel, but the committee wasn't letting her off so easily. Beth knew it wasn't Carl's taunt about looking guilty if she ran, or even Dawn's insistence that she fulfil her commitment, but the memory of Trista's worry over those phone calls that convinced her to stay put.

Something wasn't right about them and she wanted to solve the puzzle. Maybe she could pretend to forget her phone, borrow Trista's, and check the call display? Then what? Call the college and demand they deal with it? Trista wouldn't thank her for interfering.

No, better to convince Trista to seek help from the police. Maybe when Evan returned, she would suggest they talk. Thinking of Evan led Beth to wonder how Mike's father was doing and when Mike would return. Then she felt guilty for wanting to tear him away from his family.

Her cellphone rang, jogging her from her sleepy

reverie. The call display showed Mike's name. How did he always know when she needed to hear his voice?

She asked for an update on his father.

"He claims to be feeling some improvement, though his speech is slurred and he can't squeeze my hand." Mike's words dragged. He sounded discouraged and very tired.

"I spoke to Evan," Mike said.

Beth heard an edge in his voice.

"He's taking Debra to the hospital. They think it's time for the baby."

"They have another month. I hope the baby will be all right. Maybe it's a false alarm?"

"Their son was early too."

Beth heard a casual dismissal in his voice. He was upset if he didn't recognize the dangers of a premature birth.

"I wish I could be with you, but Mom won't leave the hospital and I can't abandon her. The doctor says some new process he used in the Emergency room will reverse most of the damage, but that guy looks like a kid. I can't believe he's a leading specialist in anything."

"I understand why you're not here, and I'm sure Evan and Debra do as well."

Beth refused herself the luxury of asking what Evan had told him. Mike had too many other things on his mind.

"So, the dead guy used to be your boyfriend," Mike said. "And you were meeting another fellow for breakfast. What happened, didn't your girlfriends show up?"

Beth closed her eyes and wondered why she had neglected telling Mike about Wade.

"Wade and I did go out during high school, but that was long ago."

"Evan said you walked out of a lounge with him following two seconds later. That sounds like unfinished business."

"Are you interrogating me? I thought that was Evan's job."

She didn't need Mike questioning her about her friends or her past. Damn, he was probably just feeling guilty about being so far away. She had to explain.

"Harvey, the guy who found Wade, was a good friend of mine throughout high school and long before that. Wade was not invited to the reunion, nor was he wanted and I'm not the only one who feels that way. In fact, I'm surprised at the animosity I've heard coming from others. I always thought he was well-liked."

She paused and breathed in deeply. Mike remained silent, so she started talking again to fill the empty air.

"Have you slept in the last twenty-four hours?" she asked. When he didn't answer, she continued. "That's why you're looking for an argument, but I'm not playing your game. I have a job to do if this reunion is going to be successful and since it's been nothing but one disaster after another, I have a lot of work to do."

Beth hung up before her frustration led her to say things that she would regret later.

CHAPTER TWENTY-ONE

Harvey and Trista were talking, heads close together, knees nearly touching when Beth arrived at the lounge.

Was romance growing between them? Trista flushed and laughed at something Harvey said. He took her hand.

"Taken up voyeurism, have you Beth?" Gina asked as she came up beside her. "They do make a cute couple."

"Maybe we should leave them alone?"

"Too late," Gina said, as Harvey waved in their direction.

"Good impulses aside," Gina said, as she walked toward the couple, "I need a drink and a footstool. This mall might be a shopper's heaven, but you should go into training before tackling it."

A waitress hovered nearby and Gina ordered a double scotch as she pulled out a chair. Beth, mindful of the duties still before her, asked for coffee.

"What have you two been up to this afternoon?" Gina asked, in a teasing tone.

Harvey blushed. "We played a round of miniature golf."

"And I beat him soundly," Trista added.

"You've had practice. Besides, you probably teach it at that girls' school of yours."

"Our young ladies are taught the real thing. Texans allow nothing mini into their state. Today's success was simply beginner's luck."

Harvey's grin widened as he took her hand. "Well, then we will require a rematch to see if your luck holds."

"You men do hate losing," Gina teased as she sipped her drink.

"Well, I'm pleased to announce that the reunion turnout has been spectacular and the feedback great," Beth said as she spotted Jasmine weaving her way toward them.

"I went to the spa for a wrap, massage, manicure, pedicure, and hairstyle. I feel thoroughly pampered."

"I must try that before I leave," Gina said. "All this business with Wade has me vibrating. Has anyone heard from that hunky detective?"

"Evan's wife is pregnant and may have gone into premature labour."

"So, he's off the market?"

"Definitely," Beth said.

"Do you know all the cops in town on a first name basis or just the detectives?" Gina asked, as she leaned back and crossed her ankles.

"Evan and Mike are partners."

"So you have an inside track on the investigation. Any truth to the rumour that Wade was murdered?" Gina asked as she dipped her finger into her drink, submerging an ice cube.

"I wouldn't consider asking either of them to pass

on confidential information, but I'm certain there's no suspicion of that."

"Will they let us leave on Monday?" Trista asked, in a wistful voice.

Was she looking for a reason to stay longer? Maybe that golf game had brought her and Harvey closer together than Beth had suspected.

Jasmine pulled a tiny mirror from her purse and checked her lipstick. "Has everyone been acting ridiculous around you? I've had people approach me with everything from congratulations about Wade's death to speculation about divine punishment."

"Wade's arrival stirred up lots of memories and his death at this reunion could turn him into a legend," Harvey said in a scholarly tone.

Beth wondered if he planned to write a paper about the incident. He could call it 'the effects of sudden death on the success of class reunions.' She noticed his hand was covering Trista's. From the dreamy look on his face, she figured he would remember only her.

"When I think back to the night of the accident, I remember the science fiction theory that claims the death of a butterfly can change the course of history," Jasmine said. "If that's true, think how different we would all be if Wade had been more responsible while drinking, or if Beth had ridden home with him, or if Sharon had taken the bus, or if the truck driver had been able to stop."

She stared into the distance as if seeing a different future. "Maybe if Beth had been in the car, Wade would have stopped at that sign. They would be an old married couple with lots of kids. I would be an aunt to Sharon's brood."

"I don't buy into that theory," Beth said. "I go with destiny. If Sharon hadn't died in that car, she would've greeted death in another manner. Wade and I weren't meant to be life partners or it would've happened in spite of Sharon's death.

"Do you think Trista, Gina, or Harvey had their lives dramatically altered by what happened?" Beth asked. "Would you have stayed married the first time around, or the second, or third if Sharon was alive? Would Trista have stayed in Canada? Or Gina? No. Sharon's death affected you more than the rest of us because you lost your sister suddenly and violently, but I don't believe it turned you into someone other than who you were the day before it happened."

"I don't agree with you," Gina argued.

Beth had given Gina what she loved most, a good debate topic.

"Even if you don't believe every action has a ripple effect, you have to admit that traumatic events change everyone they touch."

CHAPTER TWENTY-TWO

Harvey stretched his legs and let the conversation slide into background noise. To him it was plain: Wade had changed the lives of these women for good or bad. His disregard for the law and then his refusal to take responsibility were to blame for some of their problems.

Jasmine's anger he understood. She had insisted Sharon be treated as an equal by their group. Even in their teens, Jasmine's loving behaviour was contrary to the usual teen rejection of younger siblings. Wade had taken the object of that love away, changing Jasmine's world drastically.

Beth had had her romantic future jumbled. As a kid she had trusted too easily and believed completely in anyone she loved. Wade had destroyed those qualities. Harvey knew that in time and without therapy, she would undoubtedly find, or manufacture, some reason to turn away from Mike.

Gina had been on the outer edge of the damage, but she would retain fond memories of her recent tryst with Wade. Because their affair had ended on an up note, she would probably fantasize about the glorious future his death had cut short.

Trista was simply a sensitive person who felt her friends' pain and who had allowed it to become her own. She shouldn't have been seriously affected by

Sharon's death, but since it happened, she had locked herself away from the world.

He caressed her slender fingers. He would help her overcome her burdens, but not in a professional capacity. He wanted far more with her than a professional relationship.

Harvey thought about his conversations with class members. People confided in him, a personality flaw he sometimes regretted possessing, though it was vital in his professional life.

Arnie Hancock had told him that the football team, including Wade, had spent most of the night in a bar at the far end of the mall, hitting on twenty-year-old babes. Had Wade bothered some girl so much her irate boyfriend decided a dose of GHB was a suitable deterrent?

It would have required a large dose to cause unconsciousness and death. If Wade had been given that much in the bar, disorientation, dizziness, and vomiting would have made it difficult for him to get to Beth's room without help. He must have taken it after entering her room, but why there, why not his own room?

Harvey looked toward Trista. He found himself doing that constantly. She had changed from a nonentity into a gorgeous woman. However, her unwillingness to reveal her secrets remained firm.

Rumour had it that there had been abuse in her family. After graduating she had left town and had not returned, even for her parents' funerals. Something had torn that family apart.

But perhaps her parents were simply strict, and Trista's escape from their domination was a knee-jerk reaction that became impossible to reverse.

He forced his gaze from Trista's delicate features, not wanting his scrutiny to become apparent. Gina and Beth continued debating destiny theories, but Trista kept her opinion private. Jasmine also remained quiet, but her body language revealed she sided with Gina's ripple effect argument.

Harvey felt his gaze drift to Trista again. She smiled at him and rolled her eyes. He thought about an upcoming conference he had previously decided to miss. It was being held in Texas, not far from Trista's school. Maybe he should reconsider attending? He could visit her. It had been a long time since he had experienced such complete enjoyment in anyone's company. Perhaps after the evening banquet they would go somewhere to talk in private, maybe have a nightcap.

He noticed a lull in the debate and switched his attention back to the others.

CHAPTER TWENTY-THREE

Beth saw a girl standing in the doorway of the lounge, scanning the room's occupants. She wore jeans tucked into cowboy boots, a fleece lined jean-jacket, and carried a canvas rucksack over her shoulder. Her hair was cropped close to her skull, outlining and emphasizing her fine features.

Beth felt her breath catch in her throat: she was the girl in Wade's photo.

The girl walked toward their table, scanning each woman in turn. Beth noticed her dark eyes and the reddish tinge in her dark hair.

She addressed Trista. "Ms. Flynn, I'm Dana, your daughter."

Trista licked her lips, her gaze fastened tight to the girl. Her pale complexion faded to a sickly white. She reached for Harvey's hand and held tight.

"I told you not to come here," Trista whispered.

"How else was I going to meet you? You won't return my calls. You've given orders not to let me into your school. I had to take drastic action."

"I don't want to know you."

The girl staggered a step backward. Her expression hardened. "So you've told me, several times. If you're going to be a thorough bitch, just point me toward my father and I'll leave you alone."

Trista squeezed her eyes closed. "No," she whispered.

"I've been waiting for him. He said he would be here. He said you'd agreed we could meet."

"No. He wouldn't do that."

"How else do you think I tracked you down?"

"He's not here."

"He said he was coming."

Dana turned toward Beth, then looked at the others. "Do any of you know where I can find my father?"

Beth looked at Trista who had covered her face with her hands. Then she looked at her friends, hoping for some hint of what was happening. They met her gaze with equally puzzled expressions.

"My father," the girl repeated, looking at them as if they were either deaf or dense. "Wade Hamelin. My father. Where is he?"

CHAPTER TWENTY-FOUR

Beth swallowed half her glass of scotch. She was alone at the bar. After Dana's announcement, Harvey had taken Trista by the elbow and escorted her from the room. Dana had silently watched their departure. Jasmine had grabbed her purse and fled.

Gina recovered enough to tell Dana that Wade was dead. The girl fell into the chair Trista had vacated. Beth asked the waitress to bring her a glass of water.

"Dead," Dana said, her voice trailing into oblivion. "We talked yesterday. We'd arranged to meet this afternoon, but the snowstorm has slowed traffic on Highway 2. I knew I would be late, so I tried to call him. When he didn't answer, I phoned her. Why didn't she answer my call and tell me?"

Dana had picked up her paper coaster and began tearing tiny pieces off its edge. "Why doesn't she want to see me?"

Beth had been pondering that question for the half-hour since Gina had taken Dana away. That was when Beth had ordered a drink and given up coping with stress positively.

She couldn't believe Wade had lied to the girl, but neither could she doubt that Trista was the girl's mother. They shared too many features. But why the cruel joke of naming Wade on the birth certificate? Dana had said it was only after locating that certificate that she had tracked Wade down.

If Wade wasn't the father, then who? The girl looked to be 18 or 19, so Trista must have met the father soon after high school, probably during her first year of college.

To keep such a secret, not letting her closest friends help her through what must have been a horrible time was unbelievably selfish. Beth couldn't decide whether Trista's secrecy made her want to cry or hit something.

Then another thought intruded. Wade had allowed Dana to believe he was her father. Had he encouraged her to come to the reunion so he could expose Trista's secret? He'd said something about revenge. Had he confronted Trista? Had they argued?

No, Trista had been with Harvey when Gina saw Wade enter her room. Besides Trista couldn't hurt anyone. But then, until a few minutes ago she wouldn't have believed Trista was a mother.

Evan slid onto the stool beside her. He usually resembled an advertisement for the ultimate in men's fashion but this afternoon, though his shirt was clean, his tie straight, and his suit pressed, he looked tired and rumpled.

"Is Debra okay?" Beth asked.

"Fortunately it was a false alarm. I got her back home before the storm really got started. We're in for a good twenty centimetres."

"But you're back here, asking more questions."

"The ME agrees the death was caused by an overdose of GHB."

"He was in a bar last night. Someone could have doctored his drink, either on purpose or by accident. Maybe he went to my room looking for help?"

"He had some nasty scratches on his hand."

Beth swallowed more of her drink. "Maybe it was somewhere it shouldn't have been."

"Any idea where that was?"

"My arm," she mumbled. "I forgot to mention that he grabbed me when I was leaving."

"Important thing to forget."

"Not with everything happening. He might have been bleeding when I shook him off, but he was most certainly alive."

"Anything else you forgot to mention in all the excitement?"

"That's everything."

"We checked Wade's room. Found some fingerprints. Jog any memories?"

She finished her drink and waved for another.

"What were you looking for?"

"Something to prove how he died."

"We didn't find anything to indicate the drug was his or that he willingly took it, did you?"

"No. I just found Dana's picture. Of course, I didn't know who she was then."

"But you do now?"

"She claims Wade was her father and that Trista is her mother."

"So, is the kid lying?"

"She believes what she says."

Evan slid off the stool and rested his hand on Beth's shoulder. "I'd better talk to both mother and daughter."

"You mustn't think Trista's guilty of anything. She was with Harvey for most of the evening."

"Unless they spent the night together, she could have met Wade later. If they had a kid in common, they shared other things once upon a time," Evan said as he turned away.

CHAPTER TWENTY-FIVE

Mike slept longer than he had planned. He rolled off the sofa, showered, grabbed a cup of stale coffee and a muffin, and raced out the door into the darkness of early evening. He took a moment before putting the truck in gear to phone the hospital for an update. He was very tired of the words "no change" and "as well as can be expected."

His next call was to Beth to see how things were going at the reunion. He also wanted to apologize for anything he had said when he was too tired to think straight.

She answered, but sounded distracted. He heard the clamour of people and the thumping beat of music in the background. Her voice was slower than usual, her diction more defined, as if she was concentrating on her words. Mike wondered if she was drinking and if so, with whom.

"Am I interrupting something?"

"I'm drowning a bout of self-pity, mixed with anger and betrayal."

"What happened after we talked?"

"Evan says Debra is okay. But that Wade died of a drug overdose. I think he suspects murder."

"I'm glad to hear about Debra. The other is bad but not a surprise since he either took the drug willingly, or someone slipped it to him. Neither seem worth drowning."

"Trista has a daughter that she never told me about, and she says Wade is the father. How could she?"

Mike wondered which of Trista's sins Beth considered the worst. At least she wasn't drinking to forget her old boyfriend. Still, Mike hated being several hundred miles away while she was in a bar looking for comfort. Too many old flames were lurking around that hotel. He decided to call Evan and find out exactly where the case stood.

Beth continued speaking in a slow monotone. "The good news is that Harvey and Trista can't keep their hands off each other."

Mike felt his mood brighten, pleased that Beth thought their attraction was a good thing.

CHAPTER TWENTY-SIX

Beth studied the crowd in the bar. She recognized a few faces, but was reluctant to join any group. The waitress asked if she wanted another drink. She caught sight of herself in the mirror behind the bar.

Why was she just sitting there feeling sorry for herself? Trista owed her the truth. She slid from her chair and marched toward the elevators. Beth had to know what insanity had led Trista to record Wade's name on that birth certificate.

She had lost all interest in the reunion proceedings. She knew she would eventually change into the dress for which she had spent weeks hunting and that she would gather her notes for the evening program. It was expected of her and she always did what was expected of her.

The chatter in the elevator focused on the day's activities. She heard a boy, probably around ten years old, complaining about having to attend a dull dinner instead of a super-violent movie. She sympathized as she felt a growing desire to inflict some violence of her own.

Harvey was waiting in the hall when she stepped out of the elevator. He pulled her to the far side of the corridor. Beth read anxiety in his demeanour and worry in his eyes.

"Trista says she's staying in her room until she can

arrange a flight home. She won't tell me what's going on."

"Did she say why she made such a ridiculous claim of paternity?"

"Not a word."

"It's impossible."

Harvey pounded his fist into a nearby door frame, then turned toward her. "You always did see just the good side of Wade. Locker room gossip said he cheated on you."

Beth looked at the man who she had considered her friend. She caught his wrist before he hit the wall again. "If that's the truth, why didn't someone tell me?"

Harvey pulled his arm from her grip. "No one wanted to hurt your feelings. You were going away to university. We hoped you would forget him."

"Who is we? Who did you discuss Wade's infidelity with? Were you laughing at me for trusting someone I cared for?"

Beth blocked the impulse to run into her room and hide. She didn't want to be the subject of her classmates' pity or the butt of their jokes. She wanted to purge the entire weekend from history and start over.

"It wasn't like that. We tried to keep your faith in him intact while there was any hope of your making a life together. Remember, back then we still encouraged marriage and working out problems."

"Bull."

"Well, it's true that we thought breaking up with him was the best thing you could do. No one wanted to be the messenger, though."

Beth waited for a sense of shock and disbelief to descend. It didn't. Harvey's revelation matched Gina's hints and Carl's crude remarks. Could everyone be lying? She didn't think so. Besides after Wade's aggressive behaviour of the previous night, she wondered if she had ever really known him.

But Trista? "I can't believe Trista would betray me. Okay, I admit that she had a child without my knowing about it, but she isn't the type to betray a friend."

"Maybe it happened after you broke up with Wade?"

Had Wade sought comfort in Trista's arms during that long, lonely summer after their break-up? "She's going to tell me the truth."

"The truth might help you put this in the past where it belongs."

Beth glared at him. Did he ever stop with the psychoanalytic tripe? She brushed by him and walked toward Trista's room. She raised her fist to pound on the door, then paused, closed her eyes, and tapped gently.

"Go away Harvey."

Beth rested her forehead on the door. "It's Beth."

"Go away."

"We have to talk."

"No, we don't."

"You owe me an explanation."

"You don't want to know."

Beth drew herself upright and stepped back. "Trista if you don't open this door, I'll stand out here and pound on it until you do."

Trista hated scenes. So did Beth, but if that was what it took to get into that room, she was prepared to make a big one. As Beth raised her fist to start pounding, the door opened an inch. She pushed into the room before Trista changed her mind.

Trista staggered toward the bed, keeping her hand on the wall for support.

Doing her best to ignore the pillars, Roman statues, and hot tub, Beth turned toward Trista. She seemed tiny and frail with her shoulders hunched and her head bowed.

"I want to know what happened between you and Wade."

Trista sat cross-legged on the bed, hugging a pillow close to her chest. Tears clogged her throat and thickened her voice. Beth strained to decipher her words.

"It was a million years ago."

An image of Trista and Wade laughing at her incensed Beth; she forced herself to step back instead of reaching out to grab Trista and shake the truth from her.

"Harvey said Wade fooled around even while we were dating. Is that true?"

"I wouldn't be surprised, but if he did, it wasn't with me."

"So Dana isn't his daughter?"

Trista hugged the cushion as she jumped from the bed. She paced the room, stopping at the Jacuzzi to run her fingers over one of its fluted pillars.

Beth repeated her question.

"Are you sure you want me to answer that?" Trista asked.

"I want to know if he is Dana's father and if so, why you never told me."

Trista threw the pillow toward the window, then fell onto the bed and curled into a fetal position.

"It happened after the accident. You were being horrible to Wade, even refusing to speak to him. He came to my house and asked me to plead his case. He seemed so unhappy, that I found myself comforting him."

Beth turned toward the door. Harvey had been right. As soon as her back was turned, Wade looked elsewhere and with Trista willing, he hadn't had to search far.

Damn, she had thought Trista was more loyal than that. Beth swung around ready to tell her just what she thought of a friend who would steal her best friend's guy.

Trista lay on the bed with her arms drawn tightly around her stomach.

"I'd never really liked him." She stared at the wall, tears streaming down her cheeks. "Sure, I always thought he was sexy, but I felt uncomfortable when you weren't around. When he came by my place, he acted charming, and funny, and pathetic. I forgot to be afraid of him. He came around a few times, always wanting to talk about you. He wanted me to convince you to take him back. We never left my house, until the last time."

Beth strained to hear her whispered words. She

knelt on the carpet beside the bed, resting her hand on Trista's hair, offering comfort without knowing why.

"That time he was upset. He'd been to your house again and you'd rejected him again. He suggested we go someplace and talk without my parents hovering over us. He said he wanted to give me an argument that you would understand." Trista looked at Beth. "You remember my parents don't you? You remember how my father distrusted every boy I spoke to? And how my mother lectured me repeatedly on boys wanting only one thing?"

Trista looked away. "I should've listened to them. Wade had his driver's licence suspended after the accident, but he convinced me to drive to an isolated park so we could talk without interruption. It was a hot night near the end of July. He suggested we sit under the stars where the breeze could cool us. Then he started talking about you, but it was different that time. He was mad at you and he got angrier.

"I was afraid and suggested we leave. I said we could go for a pop and burger, my treat. That's not what he wanted. He grabbed me and started pulling at my clothes.

"I tried pushing him away, but he was too strong. When he was done, he said it was nothing personal, just a message that I should make sure you got."

Trista wiped her nose with the back of her hand. "Do you understand why I want nothing to do with that girl? I gave her up hoping to purge the memory of her conception."

Tears marked Trista's cheeks, she blew her nose fiercely. "My parents went crazy when they found out. They sent me away until she was born, then I started college—a year later than the rest of you."

"You never told me."

"You were hurting enough."

"Why didn't you press charges?"

"My parents were adamant that I say nothing. As far as they were concerned, it was my fault more than it was his. They said I'd acted like a slut and got the trouble I deserved. They wanted nothing to do with me and I obliged them by taking a job as far away as I could."

"Why did you put Wade's name on the birth certificate?"

"Why shouldn't I? Still, I never expected she would find him or me."

"Did Wade know about her?"

"Not until she contacted him. Then he tracked me to the school and demanded answers."

Trista's tears had stopped, and Beth watched defiance spring to life in her eyes.

"I told him to go to hell. He was angry that he had a kid he didn't know about. I told him that if he wanted to play father he was welcome, but that I wanted nothing to do with either of them.

"He threatened to tell the school about her. Hinted it might hurt my career if she came pounding at the door. He thought I should pay him to keep her away.

"I told him that he should be happy he wasn't in jail

and that he should thank me for not forcing him to pay child support."

She pushed herself into a sitting position and blew her nose, then tossed the tissue into the waste can. Then she slid off the bed and pulled Beth to her feet.

Trista hugged her close. "I would never have dated Wade behind your back or otherwise. If he hadn't seemed truly distraught about your rejection, I would never have been alone with him."

"You must hate me," Beth said.

"I hated him."

"I'll keep your secret, if you want me to."

Trista croaked a laugh. "Tell whoever you want. It's time the world knew what a bastard he was. I should have told twenty years ago, but I was afraid you wouldn't believe me, or worse, that you would blame me."

Beth decided they had to show the world that they were friends.

"We have half an hour before the banquet starts, do you think we can look presentable by then?"

"I don't want to face those people."

"You must and so must I. Harvey told me that everyone knew Wade cheated on me. Suddenly I'm looking at people I've known forever and wondering why they let me believe I threw away a stellar man. Wade is not getting the last laugh. I escaped a philanderer and a rapist, and you did right by a child you never wanted."

It took more convincing, but eventually Trista

agreed to go and Beth left to change into the blue silk gown she'd bought for the banquet. She had just pulled it from the closet when someone knocked on her door. Worried Trista had changed her mind, she hurried to open it. Gina stood in the hall looking gorgeous in a shimmery silver gown that fell to mid-calf and rose high on her throat. She sauntered through the door, turning her nearly bare back toward Beth, then made a production of scanning the room.

"Are they punishing you?"

"It was the only room available. Besides, I'm leaving after the banquet. Let Dawn stay if it's so important we have a committee member on site. I'm fed up with this bunch. Did you know Wade was a rat?"

"Everyone knew but you. When you were dating, you thought he was a saint. After the accident, you morphed him right into being the devil. When I met him in Bali, he was just a middle-aged Casanova romancing every female he encountered."

"But you still invited him to the reunion?"

Gina shrugged her broad shoulders and tossed her head in a defiant manner. "Tastes differ. Maybe mine runs to middle-aged cads. Besides, I just let him know the reunion was happening. If you and your little committee wanted an exclusive party, you should have inserted a note saying so inside each invitation."

"When did you know he was coming?"

"For sure? When you told me."

"Not before, not from the lists of registrants?"

"Who reads those?"

Gina sauntered to the bar and poured the contents of a miniature bottle into a water glass, then tossed in two ice cubes. With a tilt of her chin, she swallowed half the drink. "Dana's in my room. She cried herself to sleep, so I guess she'll be spending the night. Tomorrow she's going to want answers I don't have. How's Trista doing?"

"She'll survive. I'm picking her up for the banquet."

"Imagine mousy little Trista seducing Wade, then giving her kid up for adoption."

"It wasn't exactly like that."

"I always felt she was condemning me for letting custody of my kids go to their father. Her sanctimonious attitude made me feel less of a mother."

"Why did you let custody go to him?" Beth asked. "Even in California divorce judges usually favour the mother."

"What is this, confession time?" Gina downed the rest of the her drink. "Maybe it is. Nothing secret or sinister. I wasn't on drugs or fooling around with everything in pants—well not then anyway. I had spent years climbing the corporate ladder, putting my family in second place. When we parted ways, there was no contest. I was the absentee parent; he was the caretaker. Besides he married a sweet thing who was prepared to stay home and spoil the little rats."

"Couldn't you have fought, maybe found a job where you were home more?"

Gina studied the ice in the bottom of her glass. She looked toward the bar, shook her head, and placed the glass on the night table. "Now that was the root of the problem. I didn't want another job. The computer business is pulsating, and I'm good at what I do. Why should I give it up so some man can fulfil his dream? Apparently, I'm just a selfish, career-oriented bitch."

"What does that make me? I don't have kids, so I guess I have even less maternal instinct."

"What a group we are. Trista rejects hers at birth, I relinquish custody of mine, you don't bother birthing any, and Jasmine is on the eternal quest for the perfect father for hers. Maybe you were the smartest of us all."

Beth picked up her purse and with a final glance in the mirror, opened the door and waited for Gina. They would gather Trista and Jasmine, and the four of them would enter the banquet room together, presenting a solid front, just as they had throughout school.

CHAPTER TWENTY-SEVEN

Jasmine greeted them wearing a velvety green dress with a skirt that flowed to just below her knees. She closed the door behind her and they continued on to Trista's room. Trista answered so quickly Beth wondered if she had heard them coming down the hall.

She looked beautiful in her rose coloured gown. Her long black hair was piled high, a heart-shaped diamond rested between her breasts and a bracelet of tiny diamond hearts encircled her wrist.

"Harvey is meeting us outside the banquet room," Trista said, as she focused on the carpet. "I suppose you guys think I'm heartless."

Neither Gina nor Jasmine spoke. Beth placed her hand on Trista's shoulder.

"I'm not wicked. I was just too young to deal with the situation." She straightened her shoulders and looked straight at Jasmine. "You must be appalled at the thought of giving up a child."

Jasmine fiddled with the clasp of her evening bag, snapping it open, then closed, as if she hadn't heard Trista's comment. "Damn, I forgot my lipstick. You guys go ahead, I'll catch up. Just save me a spot at the table." She turned and strode away.

A sound came from Trista that was half sob and half laughter. "I guess that summarizes what she thinks of me."

"I'll talk to her; you guys find Harvey and wait for us."

Beth stretched her stride and caught up with Jasmine as she opened the door of her room. Jasmine turned and threw her arms around Beth's neck, pulling her close.

Beth fought her way free. "We thought you were angry."

"I am so damn sad for her. Without family support, she gave up the joy of raising a child. I don't know how I would have survived if it hadn't been for Tiffany. She's sustained me through every other disaster in my life."

Trust Jasmine to turn the situation into a major sobbing event. Imagine her reaction if she knew the entire truth. Damn, they had to be told so they could understand Trista's decision. Beth didn't relish spreading the word, but knew she had to start with someone.

"There's more. Trista says the sex was not consensual."

Jasmine rushed into the bathroom and splashed water on her face. As she rubbed it dry, she mumbled, "You were the only one who managed to punish him. The three-month licence suspension the court gave him was barely a hand slap. And I know he still drove, he was just too careful to get caught. Breaking off your relationship hurt him like nothing else could. It wasn't enough, but I've always been grateful you did it."

Beth thought back to that summer. She had tried to make Wade accept responsibility for his drunken actions, but he had laughed at the idea. When she begged him to apologize to Jasmine's family, he said he had nothing to apologize for. She had sworn not to speak to him until he did as she asked. He had grabbed her then too. Fortunately, her father had been around to intercede. Wade had pushed him aside and slammed out of the house. And then, he'd taken his anger out on Trista.

"It seems I remember someone who never existed."

"We should go. I've got myself under control," Jasmine said, though her eyes were red and her nose glowed under the fresh coating of powder.

As they walked, Beth asked, "Can you imagine any situation where you could have given up Tiffany?"

"No. And it's impossible to believe that now Dana has found her, Trista will reject her, not soft-hearted Trista. Remember how she used to collect stray cats and find homes for them?" Jasmine's lips trembled and Beth feared another breakdown. "Maybe we can convince Trista that Dana needs her, or at least get them speaking."

"Are we judging her too harshly? What if you hadn't been married when Tiffany was born, or worse if she had been conceived in a doomed relationship?"

"My relationship with Ralph was doomed. I just didn't know it when we married."

"I was surprised when you married him. He'd been hanging around you forever, but you never seemed interested. Then the next thing I know, I receive an announcement of your marriage."

Jasmine preceded her into the elevator, turning away as she responded. "If you are asking whether

Ralph and I conceived Tiffany before the wedding, the answer is no. I realize a lot of eyebrows rose when Tiffany was born prematurely, but people's sewer-filled minds are not my problem."

"Why did you get divorced so quickly? You were married for barely a year."

Jasmine snapped open her purse, then clicked it shut. She stared at the doors of the elevator, clicking and snapping until Beth reached out to still her hand.

Jasmine lifted her chin. "Not that it is any of your business, but after one too many Saturday nights sitting at home watching television and way too many Sunday dinners with his dear old mom, I decided the marriage was a mistake."

"At least you have Tiffany," Beth said as the elevator doors opened.

Two groups of participants waited outside the banquet room. One group had gathered close to Harvey and Trista; the other clustered in the open area nearer the conference rooms.

Beth walked into the empty space between the camps, wondering if people were casting ballots for and against Trista's mothering abilities. Some enlightened group they had turned out to be.

Trista stood against the wall. Harvey held her hand and seemed to be shielding her from harm. Gina flanked them, looking very much the knight-errant.

Dawn, dressed in black with silver earrings that matched her charm bracelet, stood in the foreground of the "against" group. Her smile was frostily superior.

Beth decided she had been one of Wade's conquests and an easy one at that.

Beth ignored the tension as she greeted Harvey. She pushed Jasmine toward Trista and was relieved when they clasped hands. At least their group was going to stand together on this.

She turned toward the ballroom door, hoping to get everyone inside so the banquet would proceed. From the corner of her eye, she saw Carl smirking as his gaze travelled over Trista. She placed her hand between Trista's shoulder blades, prepared to push her toward the ballroom if necessary.

"I don't know about the rest of you, but I'm starving," Harriet said, as she herded her husband and sons through the crowd. She patted her bulging abdomen. "There's far too much excitement at this reunion for someone in my delicate condition."

"I agree," Maggie Hartwell proclaimed, striding forward, hand raised, like a player charging the opposition. "You guys can stand around gossiping, but some of us know the value of eating a meal while it's hot."

Harvey reached for Trista's hand and held it tight. Jasmine and Gina followed and the others fell in behind.

The evening began with a speech of welcome from the committee chairman, Arnie Hancock. A moment of silence in Wade's memory followed. The meal included a bruschetta appetizer and minestrone soup; the baked chicken over rice in a mushroom sauce was followed by zabaglione. Beth was delighted to field the compliments that followed.

Then the group politely listened to Pete's rambling introduction of the teachers who had managed to attend. Ms. McKay seemed to be the only one tuned into the undercurrents flowing through the reunion. Still, most of them were long since retired, and at the hotel only to attend the banquet.

The teachers were allowed time to reminisce about milestone incidents and memorable events, including the painted goal posts when the football team won the provincials for the third year in a row, and the mascot stolen from the chess club, and the grad motto painted across the school's chain-link fence. They talked about how their favourite clubs had guided students on their paths through life.

The math teacher pointed out that of all her classes, this one had bred the most professionals. She commended Arnie for being a stellar example of what a grounding in science and mathematics could do for someone climbing the corporate ladder in the field of research and development.

The physical education teacher applauded Maggie as a person who had accepted the baton of educator and run with it, bringing the love of sports to another generation.

The principal from their era, supporting himself with two canes, told how back then, kids had been encouraged to stretch their intellect, not simply memorize facts. Nowadays, high marks counted, not the quality of the people graduating.

Ms. McKay voiced a special thank you to the class

for inviting her, saying she had especially fond memories of these students from her first year of teaching. She greeted Carl's snort and the laughter of his teammates with a coy smile.

Then Beth stood before the group longing to deliver a speech about the duty of friendship. Instead, she simply narrated the computerized slide show. To complete the program, an orchestra composed of the school's current students played while the chorus sang.

Her duties were done and the band began setting up for the dance portion of the evening. Harvey and Trista were holding hands and looked as if they were not letting go.

Jasmine excused herself, saying she had to phone Hollis.

Gina asked their muscular young waiter when he would be finished work and after receiving a satisfactory answer, ordered another drink and settled into her chair.

Beth excused herself, planning a rapid escape to her room and then home. She had done enough walking down memory lane for one reunion. Maybe she would return for the beach party, but maybe she would just hide in her house.

CHAPTER TWENTY-EIGHT

Dana sat slumped in a chair outside the banquet room. She wore the same clothes that she'd had on when Beth first saw her. The girl looked away when she realized it wasn't Trista leaving the banquet room.

The elevator doors opened. Beth stepped toward them, then changed direction and walked to Dana's chair. She couldn't walk past and leave the girl looking so desperate.

She held out her hand. "My name is Beth McKinney, and Trista is my friend. She has a good reason for not wanting to meet you."

Dana's eyes were huge with suppressed tears, her nose red from crying. Beth let her hand drop to her side.

"We communicated by e-mail, you know. My dad and me. Did you know him?"

"Until recently, I thought I did. What did he tell you about Trista?"

"He promised to tell me everything when we met face-to-face." She bent forward and hugged her knees to her chest. "I guess that won't happen now."

A group of boisterous conventioneers wandered into the hall, bringing a gaiety that struck a sour note. Beth waited for their overly loud laughter to fade as they walked toward the elevators.

"Did any of you like him?" Dana asked. "I've

talked to people, but it's like they're dealing with some major issue instead of ancient history."

Ancient history? How do you resolve a hurt that is covered by twenty years of scar tissue?

"Walk with me and I'll tell you what I can. It might not be what you want to hear, but if you're certain you want the truth, I can tell you as much as anyone."

Dana grabbed her rucksack and jumped to her feet. The eagerness Beth saw on her face was almost unbearable. How could she edit the facts to make them easier for the girl to hear?

They walked past other banquet rooms, catching threads of music drifting through the open doorways. When they came to the spiral staircase leading to the main floor, Beth studied their fractured image in the dozens of mirrors encircling the stairwell.

Dana's fingers drummed on the rail as her impatience grew. Beth told Dana how the group of friends had gone through school together and how she and Wade had met on the first day of high school. Wade had never tried to fit into her existing group of friends that included Harvey, Trista, Jasmine, and Gina. She stressed that Wade had shown no interest in Trista.

Beth saw questions in Dana's eyes. She would answer them, but knew Dana needed some background information if she was to understand Trista's rejection. Beth told her how the friends had gone everywhere together, though she stressed that she and Wade had always paired up.

She told Dana about the athletic awards Wade had

won and about his popularity. Then she told Dana about Trista's shyness. About how she was always willing to offer a sympathetic shoulder.

Finally, she told Dana about the night of the drunken accident, and Sharon's death.

"After that, our group fell apart. I went east to college, trying to escape the guilt I felt. Survivor guilt." She looked at their broken reflections, repeated until they seemed as unreal as the memories she was bringing into the harsh light.

"Gina left town for the west coast and Trista went south. Jasmine married that October. Harvey started a pre-med program."

Dana shrugged her rucksack higher onto her shoulder, then bent far over the rail, as if contemplating a swan dive that would end four floors below.

"The way you tell it, Trista and Wade could not be my parents, but that's what the birth certificate said, and Wade verified it."

Beth heard restrained anger in her tone and hurried to finish her story. "In the last two days I have learned that Wade wasn't monogamous. I was so busy earning good marks, keeping up with my extracurricular activities, and holding down a job, that I never realized Wade was unfaithful back then."

Beth studied Dana. She looked strong enough to handle the rest of the tale.

"This evening I learned something else. Apparently, Wade approached Trista when I refused to speak to him. He took advantage of her innocent, trusting nature. It's called date rape now, though I don't agree with using a qualifier."

The girl's thin shoulders hunched. Beth wondered if she could have coped with a similar disastrous revelation at Dana's age.

Dana stumbled down the stairs. Beth followed. Once in the mall, the dance music left far above, Dana lurched toward a bench. She lay on her side and curled into a fetal position. With her hands clutched tight between her knees, she stared straight ahead. "No wonder she doesn't want me."

Beth knelt beside the bench, stroking Dana's hair in the same way she had stroked Trista's only hours before. These two needed each other, and she was going to get them to connect.

"Trista isn't a bad person, but she's having trouble dealing with one of life's curve balls. It's been a rough weekend. We arrived hoping to renew friendships and have instead been ambushed by catastrophe. Let's talk to Trista and see if we can salvage one good thing from this reunion."

Dana's face twisted into a mutinous expression, one Beth had seen Wade wear numerous times.

Dana stumbled to her feet. "I'm leaving. Tell her not to worry; I won't bother her again. Tell her that I understand why looking at me makes her want to puke."

Dana's snort of manic laughter landed like acid on Beth's ears. She had revealed too much. Abandoning the girl to her misery would be heartless. With an arm tight around Dana's shoulders, Beth turned them toward the stairs. Dana didn't protest.

Beth had only a vague plan in mind, but if it worked, perhaps Trista and Dana could find a starting point.

The dance floor was crowded when Beth returned, towing Dana behind her. Beth saw fear spread across Trista's face as they approached, but steeled herself. She pulled out a chair and pushed Dana into it. Then she sat between mother and daughter.

Beth grabbed Trista's hand and held tight. "I've told her the whole story and half of our life histories as well. Now she thinks she's worthless and that no one wants her. You're her mother and a teacher. Help her through this."

Beth looked at the faces of the people sitting around the table. Gina had forgotten her waiter for the moment and was watching Trista like a psychic sending a message. Harvey tightened his grip on Trista's forearm and leaned over to speak into her ear. Some of the tension drained from her expression.

Trista looked directly at Dana for the first time, then she turned back toward Harvey. He nodded. She pulled her hand from Beth's grip and touched Dana's fingers. "I can only promise to try."

CHAPTER TWENTY-NINE

Once Trista agreed to talk to her daughter, Beth decided to spend the night at the hotel. Perhaps the jinx had lifted and she could enjoy a final day with her friends at the poolside picnic. Maybe she would even fulfil her entire commitment and stay around for the dinner theatre.

Looking at her classmates, Beth realized how many ways there were to live a life. Why had she chosen one so sheltered and boring? She should throw caution to the winds, take risks, live for the moment.

And repent at leisure. Beth tried to ignore the warning thought, but found the euphoria she had felt at Trista's capitulation evaporate. She had dug her little groove and was comfortable with it. Climbing over the edge might be exciting, but the walls were very high.

She watched as Trista and Dana made a few fumbling attempts at conversation. Trista looked toward Harvey, as if seeking his counsel. He said something and she stood, motioning for Dana to follow.

Beth watched the two women leave the room, each carefully avoiding contact with the other.

"Well, that's one problem on the way to resolution," Gina quipped. "Now we just have to deal with the fallout from Wade's death. Any news on that front Beth?"

Beth wanted to keep the atmosphere upbeat and

decided giving them some basic facts and her theory of events shouldn't cause a problem.

"The police know he died of a drug overdose. That particular drug is unpredictable and even habitual users can miscalculate. I'm sure their finding will be accidental death."

Harvey left a short time later, having promised to drive a friend to the airport. The snow was still falling, but he assured Beth it was nothing his SUV couldn't handle.

Others left then too. Some wanted to enjoy the luxurious fantasies they were paying for in the theme rooms. Others wanted to get home before the snowplows took to the roads and tied up traffic.

Gina slipped a note to her waiter and then said to Beth, "What did the cops really say?"

"I told you."

"You told us the party line. Now give me the dirt. What drug did he take?"

"GHB. It's . . ."

"I know what it is. It's a libido booster among other things."

"Do you think he took it on purpose?"

"I saw him going into your room with a woman. It follows," Gina said.

"Do you remember anything more about her? The colour of her clothes, jewellery, her voice, nail polish? Evan wants to find her."

Gina pursed her lips. "Just that she was female."

"Why are you so certain?"

"Do you think I can't tell the difference?" Gina asked. "Speaking of which, I told Carlo to meet me in my room after his shift, which ends any minute now. I best go freshen up."

Beth wondered why Gina needed a younger man. There were plenty of men their age roaming the halls of the hotel. If she wanted companionship, wouldn't one of them suit her better?

Jasmine had returned from her phone call and worked the room until she took root beside Dawn. Beth wondered what conversational middle ground the class Pollyanna and a sarcastic pessimist could find. Maybe Jasmine was seeking tips in handling crowd control—Hollis might desire that in the wife of a politician. Or perhaps they were discussing investment opportunities. Jasmine was reputed to have done well from all her divorces, and Dawn had her lotto winnings.

Suzanne, spectacular in a black, sequin-covered shirt, and hip-hugging jeans had left immediately after the program finished. Beth watched as she rejoined her group, towing three middle-aged males behind. So the rumours were true and that group did use the reunion as an excuse for a couple of days of unencumbered sex.

Katy Starr looked up as one of the men pulled out the chair beside her. She shook her head, then glanced toward Beth, meeting her gaze for a fraction of a second before turning away. In that instant, Beth saw embarrassment and guilt. Was she regretting deserting her sick husband and handicapped son for a weekend of leisure? Damn, life wasn't fair for mothers. You were either guilty of neglect or busy beating yourself into a bout of depression.

Suzanne leaned toward Katy, as if pleading with her. Katy pushed her chair back and fled the room. Rhonda Peters turned toward the deserted fellow. The band stopped playing just as she spoke, carrying her voice to the corners of the room letting everyone know she had invited him to join them, even if Katy was playing the good mother. He looked at her for a second, then fastened his attention on the sparkling lariats outlining Suzanne's breasts.

Maggie Hartwell tugged her husband over to Beth's table. In her booming voice, she confided that their daughter was having a wonderful experience and Maggie could not believe how happy she was.

It reminded Maggie of the time they'd gone to a midnight drive-in for Monica's birthday. Beth must remember the fun they'd had on that dusk 'til dawn excursion.

Beth tried looking as if she remembered the occasion, but nothing flowed into those blank spaces of her mind. Her lapse of memory didn't matter, Maggie insisted, because Monica had only been at the school for a few months. What was important was how much fun Jessie was having collecting e-mail addresses right, left, and centre. Maggie said they should have a reunion next year instead of waiting the usual five.

Beth kept a smile pasted on her lips while silently vowing not to become involved with another reunion, ever. She submitted to another of Maggie's bear hugs, surprised to discover she no longer felt uncomfortable with the public display.

Janice Tyler danced in the arms of her girlfriend and smiled serenely at the shocked expressions they provoked. When they returned to their table, Beth joined them.

When Bobbie Dillan wandered over with her friend in tow, Beth caught herself wondering if the boyfriend used to be a woman. She cut off the thought and felt ashamed it had even popped into her mind.

Some hint of it must have reflected in her expression because Bobbie scowled at her. Beth wiped the rogue smile from her lips and wondered what Mike would think of this group. He favoured traditional lifestyles. Besides he was a cop, and a man, and Janice made it clear she could tolerate few of either species.

Bobbie said she just hated cops, male or female. It seemed they had hassled her when she worked the streets. Her day job as an architectural design technician paid well, but not enough to cover a complete sex change.

Beth enjoyed their conversation, but her few hours of sleep the previous night and the stress of the day had her dozing.

Then Bobbie said, "I remember in high school Wade drank kegs, but last night he wasn't keeping up."

Her words jolted Beth awake. "You saw him last night?" she asked

"Yeah. He was with the jock crowd at the country western bar down the mall. It's supposed to have the best dance floor in the province."

"They were drinking heavily?"

"Downing brews and staring at a few sexy young things."

Beth noticed her long slender fingers. What characteristic would make an arm seem feminine?

"What was Wade drinking?" Beth asked.

"Well, it wasn't beer, which surprised me. He seemed the beer type."

"Did you see anyone around their table?" Beth asked.

"We were busy two-stepping, not paying attention to them. You think someone doctored his drink?"

"It happens," Beth said.

"Never leave your drink unattended, blah, blah, blah. I'm careful about open bottles and free drinks, but if you do everything the authorities recommend, you end up carrying your own water bottle everywhere just like Dawn does," Janice interjected.

"Don't start picking on Dawn again," Bobbie said. "She's been helping out everywhere this weekend. I think you owe her one, Beth. She spent half an hour convincing Wade to stay away from you and Trista."

"And she's kept a close eye out ensuring that everyone is having a good time. I saw her grab a couple of stragglers and point them toward the action. Most everyone is mingling now."

"Especially Carmen McKay," Janice interjected, her voice dripping with scorn. "She couldn't keep her eyes off Wade. My guess is she was remembering other times they'd mingled."

Ms. McKay and Wade? It wasn't possible. Beth felt her stomach flip flop. "She was our science teacher."

"Wade met her on the sly for half of our final year."

Would it never end? Beth wanted to crawl away.

"Don't worry, Beth," Janice patted her shoulder. "It wasn't as if they publicized it, and you could tell Wade really loved you. He was just a slimy male who needed a variety of sexual partners. You were the only female he ever treated decently."

Janice's words didn't help her self-esteem.

Bobbie stretched her well-muscled arms, then put her hand under her escort's elbow and helped him stand. "Well, I can't speak for the rest of you, but I turn into a pumpkin at two AM."

Beth was surprised to find theirs was the last table occupied. The wait staff had cleared the other tables and the band was packing up.

She rode the elevator to her room. The traffic signals were blinking and so was the message light on the phone.

"Harvey here. Just confirming that we're meeting at 8:30 in the lobby."

Beth debated asking for a wake up call, but decided her internal clock would wake her well before then.

Gina's breathless message followed. "I've remembered why I thought the person was female. Why did you turn off your cellphone and why am I talking to this machine? You'll love this. I've got to see your face when I tell you." The message ended.

Beth phoned Gina's room, but no one answered.

She retraced her steps to the ballroom, hoping Gina had gone searching for her. The room was empty. She debated knocking on Gina's door, then remembered Carlo. Gina had probably been distracted by his arrival. The morning would be soon enough to learn what she had remembered.

CHAPTER THIRTY

Beth's sleepy greeting told Mike he had woken her. "The party went well, I take it?" he asked.

"It was great, but I didn't get to bed until nearly three."

"Well, you can go back to sleep now that I've heard your voice."

"How's your father?"

"They say he's going to recover to almost one hundred percent."

"So his speech is going to be okay?"

"It's slurred, but the doctor thinks it will return to normal. His paralysis is already lessening."

"That's a relief."

"He's pretty scared and depressed. We're attending a training session with a home care nurse and a physiotherapist on Monday, so I won't be back to Edmonton until at least Tuesday."

"You should stay as long as they need you."

"I miss you," Mike said, half wishing she would ask him to return.

"It's been crazy around here," she said instead. "Wait until I tell you about my classmates. They've turned into an interesting group."

"I wish I'd been there."

"You would have been bored. I think all the spouses and significant others fell into a stupor, or drank themselves into one."

"I'll make it up to you. We'll invite the bunch of them to our wedding."

"I doubt my backyard will hold them all, even the best of them. Did I tell you Trista has a daughter?"

Mike pretended not to notice the rapid change of topic. After all, they were both satisfied with their current lives and neither was prepared to make concessions. Sometimes a week went by without their seeing each other. At least they kept in touch by cellphone.

Beth had once asked him to move into her huge two-storey house. She'd argued that if they lived in the same place, they could at least wave as one walked in the door and the other out. He refused to take that path, because he prided himself on learning from the mistakes of others and he knew she quickly tired of roommates.

Sometimes he caught himself wishing they had eloped last summer. He'd had her convinced. They had the licence, but at the last moment, they'd decided family and friends would be hurt at being excluded.

When Beth paused after telling him about Bobbie's sex change, Mike asked if she had talked to Evan about the investigation.

"Not since his update on Debra," she said. "I'm hoping this thing fades away to nothing. Even if Wade overdosed, it was probably an accident, or some joker in the bar. We talked about it last night and everyone agreed they were the most likely scenarios."

"You think he left his drink unattended?"

"Sure. Guys don't worry about rape, just us women.

I've got to go. Breakfast with Harvey, then I'm meeting Lorelei to go over the arrangements for the poolside picnic.

"Oh, and Gina remembered something about the woman she saw with Wade. I've got to track her down. Gotta go. See you Tuesday."

Mike caught his reflection in the mirror and smoothed the scowl from his face. He intended to meet Harvey as soon as he got back to Edmonton. Beth had been cool since she'd reconnected with the guy.

CHAPTER THIRTY-ONE

Harvey waited for Beth in the quiet of the hotel lobby. Only a few families were roaming so early on a Sunday. His trip to the airport had been exhausting, with fifteen centimetres of snow and visibility down to nil, but the flight had boarded on time.

He was tired but eager to get Beth alone for the selfish reason of talking about Trista. He had hoped someone would fill him in during the banquet, but it hadn't worked that way and he was desperate to know what was going on.

Beth exited the elevator yawning, but looking more relaxed than he had seen her all weekend. Her short curly hair was damp and she had foregone makeup.

"Let's get out of this hotel," he said as he dragged her through the corridor, dodging the small group gathered near the chapel, slowing only to examine a bookstore display as they walked down the mall.

With most of the stores opening at noon on Sunday, he could finally appreciate the size of the mall without the crowds that made it seem cramped.

"If Mike hadn't called and talked the sleep out of me, I might have rolled over and ignored your invitation."

"You slept poorly?"

"Nothing like crawling into the back of a pickup for a good night's rest."

"You didn't!"

"It was the only room they had available. Still, it was a comfortable mattress and after I phoned the desk to find out how to turn those damned traffic lights off, I caught some sleep."

As they passed through the food fair, Beth inhaled the scent of fresh croissants. "I need coffee, soon."

Harvey kept her walking until they arrived at a café on dimly lit Bourbon Street.

"I will probably never discover everything this mall has to offer," Beth said after they were seated, with coffee poured and breakfast placed before them.

"And if you did, some store would close or move and you'd have to start over."

"And even when they don't move, I need a map to find them again. Thank goodness they've got it in an electronic format now."

Harvey studied Beth across his plate of pancakes and sausages. Maple syrup mingled with butter and spilled onto the plate. Beth poked at her blueberry muffin and fruit cup, as if uncertain of her appetite.

"So Harvey, old man, why are we breakfasting together? Does it have to do with Dana?"

"It's really none of my business . . ."

"That favourite line. I thought you could do better than that."

He looked at her, surprised to hear the teasing tone in her voice. She'd been so focused all weekend he'd assumed she had lost her sense of humour.

"What, you're not here to ask about Trista and her daughter?"

Harvey felt himself blush. He speared a chunk of pancake, studying his forkful as he debated admitting to such curiosity. "You may have noticed that I'm fond of Trista."

Beth's grin made him feel very transparent. He was used to reading others, not to being read. He cleared his throat and started again. "We've hit it off rather well, but with Dana's appearance yesterday I thought I needed guidance about what to say and do so I don't mess up."

Beth's grin disappeared. She lifted her mug with both hands and keeping her gaze fastened on his, told him a story he wished he didn't have to hear. Why was it that tragedy so often followed the same story line?

Beth signalled the waitress for more coffee. "I feel like hell that we missed seeing something so disastrous. Maybe we could have helped her through it."

"She was right to give Dana up for adoption," Harvey said.

Beth bit into the second half of her muffin, chewing it slowly as though she found it unpalatable. "So, how do we approach her today?"

"Let's just wait and see how they managed last night."

Beth's earlier grin returned as she studied him. "Do you think you'll be seeing Trista after this weekend?"

"There's a conference in Texas next month that I should attend. If memory serves, it's being held near her school. Perhaps I'll make a side trip. Just to see how things are going with her. This meeting with Dana should have worked through her defences by then and she might need to talk to someone."

"You are indeed a kind fellow."

"Establishing a mother-daughter relationship is a major life change."

"And you really do like her."

Harvey looked at his uneaten pancakes. He poured syrup over the forkful he'd cut much earlier. "Is that a problem?"

"Not as far as anyone who has seen you two together is concerned. I wish you well."

Harvey felt his shoulders relax, even though he caught a whisper of sadness running through Beth's words. Harvey knew the problems that led to chronically catastrophic relationships. He had seen a number of people, most often women, fighting against committing to a marriage or long-term arrangement. Trista had been like that, but he felt sure she would change once she fully reconciled with Dana.

He hoped he would be lucky enough to find someone to spend his life with. Once, long ago he'd thought he had found the right person. That marriage had failed, thankfully before there were kids to worry about. An image of Trista popped into his thoughts, but he knew it was far too early to even think such things.

Beth leaned back in her chair and took her coffee mug in both hands. "So, how do you think she and Dana managed last night?"

"However it went, just facing the girl was a major step forward. I'm impressed with her courage, especially in light of the story you told me. However, I know a few cases like theirs—the success rate is low."

Beth placed her mug on the table and reached for her purse. "I have to talk to Lorelei about the set-up for our poolside buffet."

Harvey remained in his chair, unwilling to end their camaraderie. Beth might have the day planned, but he had little to do but people watch.

"I booked a lesson with a golf pro," Harvey said.

"You're determined to beat Trista?"

"At least the next time we play, I will provide some competition."

"You two make a good match."

"Too early to tell."

"I can spot a couple with sticking power."

"What about you and Mike? Any sticking power there?"

Beth sighed and turned toward him. "Some days, I think so, but I'm sure if I stall long enough I'll find some reason to run screaming into the sunset."

Just as Harvey feared, Beth was aware of her problem and chose to do nothing to correct it. He decided to bend his rule and nudge her into action. "Do you want to find a flaw in him or just confirm that you're unworthy of a permanent relationship?"

"Permanence is not in the cards for some people. Every time I start thinking about marriage something happens, they join the priesthood, or want a dozen kids, or bankrupt my parents. Marriage talk brings bad karma my way."

"That sounds ominous. If Mike is smart, he won't give you time to vanish."

Harvey watched her amble toward the hotel. He was going to find time to talk to Mike and tell him that if he was waiting for her to conquer her phobia of commitment, he might be in for a long wait.

CHAPTER THIRTY-TWO

Evan intercepted Beth as she browsed through a kitchen gadget store on her way back to the hotel. He looked as if he was surviving without sleep.

"Is Debra all right?" Beth asked.

Evan offered her a chocolate cigar decorated with a pink bow.

"That's great, Evan. Everything went smoothly?"

"Couldn't have been easier, though Debra disagrees."

"The baby is all right, even though she was early?"

Evan rubbed the back of his neck. "A bit smaller than Kenny, but the doctor says she is perfect in every way."

"That's wonderful. When can I see them?"

"They'll be home tomorrow, but give us a couple of days to readjust."

"I'm happy for you," Beth said, though looking into Evan's bloodshot eyes, she felt the announcement wasn't his only reason for being there. "Why aren't you with them?"

"I have to ask you some questions."

She studied his expression. "Can it wait until the reunion is finished?"

"I'm afraid not. You were with that Harvey guy again, right? Seeing a lot of him aren't you?"

"He's an old friend."

"His practice is in town, why haven't you linked up before?"

Beth wondered where his questions were leading. Could he be protecting Mike's interests?

"Twenty years is a long time and Edmonton is a big city. I've lost contact with lots of my classmates."

"But you aren't breakfasting with them."

"Is there a point to this, Evan?"

"I don't want to see Mike hurt."

He was playing the protector. What absolute nerve he had. "Let me worry about my relationship with Mike."

"He's my partner."

Beth inhaled deeply and placed her hand on Evan's arm. "Trust me, I do not intend to hurt him. Now, if that's all you wanted." She let her sentence hang.

Evan's unsettling stare didn't waver. She felt guilty.

"The stuff that killed Wade was used as a growth hormone before it was banned. Your parents run a gym, did they ever catch someone using it?"

"Not that I know of."

"Maybe Wade took it to suppress his inhibitions? Was he normally a shy, repressed person?"

"Not the Wade I remember."

"It's available through the Internet," Evan said staring at her as he spoke, as if expecting some violent reaction.

She felt a librarian-style compulsion to help him find the information he was seeking. "A computer search might work if you can find the seller and access his records."

Evan continued staring at her, as if willing her to think of some obvious truth.

"Did Wade buy the stuff?" she asked. "Did you find some in his belongings?"

"Someone phoned the tip-line last night. Told us where to find some packaging from an Internet supplier of the drug."

"That's great. So now you know where Wade got it."

"We found the container in a garbage can behind your house. The order was sent to you, care of a postal box."

Beth sat on the nearest bench. She often ordered merchandise through the Internet, but never any type of drug.

"You can't seriously believe I did this? Why would I want to hurt someone I haven't seen in twenty years?"

He waited for her answer, probably hoping she would start talking and incriminate herself. Thank goodness, Mike wasn't involved with this investigation.

But it was impossible. She knew she hadn't ordered the stuff, much less given it to Wade. She thought for a few minutes, feeling the weight of Evan's silence.

"When was it ordered," Beth finally demanded.

"About a month ago. Why did you order it? Were you experimenting? Did someone at the gym need it? Maybe your psychiatrist friend wanted it to help a patient, but didn't want a trail leading back to him?"

"Anyone could have ordered that stuff using my name. It would have been easy."

"Not only your name, but your credit card, and your e-mail account."

"Identity theft has to be the answer. Someone got my Social Insurance Number and applied for a credit card in my name. Companies are always sending out credit card forms. If someone used my name and a postal box and paid the bills, I would never know."

"And your e-mail address?"

"They could have set up another address using my name."

"Why go to that much trouble?"

"You said the stuff is illegal."

Evan's blank expression hid his feelings, but Beth felt disapproval seeping from his pores. He actually thought she was using the stuff and probably cheating on Mike as well.

"This is awful for you isn't it? You think I'm guilty, but you want to protect Mike. Are you arresting me?"

He stared down the mall. When he looked at her again, his lips were twisted into a pained smile. "I don't believe you hurt anyone, but I've got to tell you this looks bad. Is your mail program password protected?"

"Of course, and my house is monitored by a security system and the only person who has a house key, other than Mike, is my cleaning lady and she is computer illiterate. There are, however, ways to hack into someone's computer from offsite, though I don't think I have friends or enemies who have the know-how to do it."

"You better think hard, because someone has gone

to a lot of trouble to make it look as if you ordered that drug."

"Why? I don't have enemies."

"Wade died in your bed from a quick-acting drug. That's the first thing pointing at you. Then, someone gives us evidence that points right at you. My guess is that someone is framing you."

"You think someone drove to my house in that storm, just to put an envelope in my garbage can?"

"There were no footprints in the snow and the envelope was near the bottom of the can. This wasn't a spur of the moment plan."

Beth stared at the growing number of shoppers. "Someone hates me that much?"

"Luckily, he was seen only minutes before your house alarm was deactivated." His stare held hers with a piercing intensity. "Unless your friend lied or you had an accomplice, you couldn't be in two places at once."

Evan closed his notebook. "Look, I'm sure someone wants to hurt you. I've arranged for an office where we can try to figure out who and why, in private."

CHAPTER THIRTY-THREE

The office Evan had commandeered held a desk and a visitor chair. He leaned across the desk, his recorder turned on and notebook open.

"First, who had access to your hotel room?"

"It was the reunion committee's designated meeting spot and storage room. Friday, most of the members were in there at one time or another. I authorized Lorelei to hand out key cards as needed."

"No one but committee members, then?"

"I had an extra keycard for Mike."

Evan looked up from his notes. "You returned it to the desk?"

"No, the last time I noticed it, it was on the dresser."

"We didn't find it. Anyone else?"

"My friends, Gina, Trista, and Jasmine, but they wouldn't have taken it."

"We're making a list of people to talk to, not accusing anyone. Any of those people been to your house?"

"The committee met there a couple of times. Trista stayed with me last summer."

"So any of them hate you?"

"Wade is the one who died. Shouldn't you ask if they hated him?"

"Maybe the plan was to get a bottle of that drug into your room, then slip you an overdose. If you were found with it in your system, a supply close by, and the shipping package in your garbage—well, we wouldn't have looked elsewhere."

"Then why kill Wade?"

"Maybe the plan changed when he arrived. He could have been a secondary target, or just a way to make you suffer. Anyone have a grudge against you both?"

Beth thought of Sharon's death. "If you look back twenty years, it's possible."

"Sometimes the need for revenge simmers for years. Still, let's look at more recent events first." He paced the small room. "Successful people can be targets of jealousy."

"That's silly." But the heightened colour in his face made Beth wonder if he was expressing his own feelings. "Why don't you just trace the call?" she asked.

"Tip-lines make a point of not tracking calls."

"It wasn't one of my friends."

"Too bad your buddy, Gina, didn't get a better look at the woman with Wade."

Beth snapped her fingers. "I forgot. She phoned me last night, said she remembered something."

"What?"

"She left a message, but didn't give me details and I haven't talked to her since."

"What did she say, exactly."

"That she remembered why she thought the person was a woman. Said she wanted to see my face when she told me."

"Like perhaps it wasn't a woman?"

"Hold on. She didn't say that."

"Did she imply that she'd been mistaken? Why would you identify someone you could hardly see as a woman?"

Beth thought for a moment. "Their arm would be slender."

"Your little psychiatrist has skinny arms. He sure didn't like Wade."

Beth glared, bothered by his smug tone. Evan would love to pin this on someone he saw as Mike's competition. "Maybe they wore nail polish?"

"The sex change woman has long nails."

"Bobbie would have hauled him in by the collar, but I don't think she's Wade's type."

"That drug blurs the whole gender issue."

"Bracelets are still a female thing," Beth said.

"Lots of people around here wearing them?"

Beth searched her memory. "Probably. This is ridiculous. Ask Gina what she meant, I have to get to my meeting with Lorelei. We're just going to have to wait until the reunion is over to figure this out."

"Someone's out to get you."

"To embarrass me maybe, but they screwed up and now Wade is dead."

"Be careful. They may still be looking to hurt you. I told Debra I'd be right back, four hours ago, so I'm off to see our lovely little daughter now. I'll come back to speak to your friend as quickly as I can."

CHAPTER THIRTY-FOUR

Beth used the few minutes before her meeting with Lorelei to hurry to the fish tanks on the second level. She had to think and found watching the vibrantly coloured saltwater fish with their hypnotic movements therapeutic.

A spiny fish floated toward the top of the tank, creating bubbles as it searched the surface for food. Its only concern was satisfying its immediate needs. It knew its place in the food chain—a meal for those higher and predator of those lower. It knew its enemies, she didn't.

Beth shook her head, refusing to believe that anyone would want to hurt her. Maybe Evan had her overanalyzing and Wade's death was the accidental overdose it seemed.

Evan was in a spot. It was obvious he was treating her with more consideration than he would any other suspect. If Mike were in town, he would have to withdraw from the case. Not that Mike would do that willingly, he would try to protect her and maybe damage his career in the process.

A group of kids raced toward the fish tank, yelling and jostling her aside. She stepped back, letting them have a clear view of the beautifully ugly fish.

She had to step out of Mike's way. She had to break off their engagement before she ruined his career. When he returned, she would tell him.

With her decision made, Beth turned away from the hypnotic movements of the fish. Though it was only ten-thirty and many of the stores were still closed, the crowds had arrived.

As she hurried to her meeting with Lorelei, Beth again dialed Gina's room. There was still no answer.

CHAPTER THIRTY-FIVE

Lorelei was dealing with a problem customer when Beth entered the lobby. She tilted her head, indicating that Beth should wait in her office.

"Sorry I was late," Beth said, when Lorelei entered.

"There's time. It's just small details."

They dealt with business quickly, then Lorelei leaned back in her chair. "Any feedback I should pass onto management?"

"The part of the reunion you organized has gone wonderfully."

"Someone dying usually tends to spoil the fun."

"I can't reach Gina and I need to talk to her. She was meeting Carlo, one of your waiters, last night. Can you find out where I can reach him?"

"I'll check his schedule." After a brief phone conversation, Lorelei said, "He's in the dining room working the Sunday brunch. He'll be along in a minute."

A few minutes later Carlo strutted into the room, giving Lorelei a quick glance before focusing on Beth.

"Gina's not answering her phone. Do you know where she is?" Beth asked.

"We never connected. She'd hung a 'do not disturb' sign on her door. I knocked anyway. No answer."

"Lorelei, can we check her room?" Beth asked, as all the niggling worries she'd kept pushing away sprang into the foreground.

The sign was still on the door when Lorelei opened it. She called out as she stepped inside. Then again as she flicked on the lights.

Beth trailed behind her.

"Help me," Lorelei called.

Beth hurried to her side. Gina bobbed face down in the Jacuzzi. The water was tinged red. Her hair was matted with blood. Together they pulled her out and laid her on the floor. Beth started CPR, though she knew Gina had been dead for hours.

"I'll call the police," Lorelei said. Then after hanging up, "The hotel has met every safety standard. Do you think she was drunk and passed out?"

Beth looked around the room. Suitcase open, shopping bags stacked beside it. Gina's clothes lay on the bed. A black matte statue on the dresser next to a perfume bottle. Beth stepped forward.

"Beth," Evan said touching her arm. "I came looking for her too."

Beth pointed toward the perfume bottle. "Gina never wore perfume. Too afraid of upsetting business contacts."

"GHB container?"

"It would clear customs."

"Maybe there was no other woman. She could have been a user, even given it to Wade," Evan said.

Beth pointed toward the statue sitting on the dresser. "Someone could have hit her with that."

"Or she could have slipped in the Jacuzzi. No theorizing until the scene has been processed."

"Beth," Lorelei called from the doorway. "I've called your committee people. They're meeting us downstairs."

"Why?"

"They have to be told the details before your party."

Beth stared at her, wondering what she was talking about. Gina was dead, they couldn't have a party.

But Arnie had already gathered and briefed the other members.

"We kept going after Wade kicked," Carl said. "That set a precedent, so we have to have this beach thing."

"Besides, we've paid for the buffet and people have to eat," Dawn pointed out. "We can make it a sort of memorial for them both. People might like that because who knows when, or where, their funerals will be."

"Next, you'll be saying it's what Gina would have wanted," Beth said.

"No," Dawn replied. "She was way too selfish for that. She'd have wanted us to go into mourning for a full year."

Beth took a step forward. "I've had enough of your putting down my friends."

"Maybe you better rethink who your friends are," Carl said. "From what I hear, someone is pointing the cops your way. Maybe it was Gina? She had a hankering for Wade. Woman scorned, you know."

"Then why is she dead?"

"Mood swings made her suicidal? Or hey, maybe

she saw you hauling Wade into your room and threatened to tell your fiancé, so you stuck her head under water to keep her quiet?"

Carl was wrong, Gina had died because someone didn't want her telling what she'd remembered.

"Let's go ahead with that beach party," Beth said as she fled the office.

CHAPTER THIRTY-SIX

The humid, hot air wrapped around Beth like a quilt on a cold night. Far above the pool, the sky stretched clear and blue. The rim of snow outlining the glass-domed ceiling was the only reminder of yesterday's storm. Calypso music drifting through the palm trees reminded her of the Caribbean.

Beth wore a bathing suit with a wrap-around skirt, though her inclination had been to add a heavy sweater. Something about lounging around open water in Edmonton, in November, demanded at least a sweater, if not a parka.

She placed her glass of lemonade on the table beside her chair and stretched her arms high over her head, then shifted to a more comfortable position.

Palm Cove, the private function area reserved for her reunion group, was in a quiet corner of the Waterpark. In the distance, she could see the lookout that allowed shoppers to stare into the grotto, like spectators at a zoo.

She listened to the chatter rumbling around her—people were slightly subdued, but life must go on, right? She closed her eyes on the tears that threatened, and then exhaled slowly.

When she opened them again, Beth saw Trista and Dana walking side-by-side past the cabanas, the refreshment stand, and the lounge. They didn't touch, but looked comfortable in each other's presence.

As they approached the grotto, Trista waved at Beth. They veered toward her, taking only a few steps before Dana pointed toward a monstrous water slide. She handed Trista her tote bag and rushed toward the screams of enjoyment.

"Things went well?" Beth asked, as Trista drew a chair close.

"She's a good kid who was lucky enough to be raised by good people. I guess I shouldn't have shut her out like I did."

"It was the right thing to do, though I'm glad she's hunted you down. You deserve a daughter who is as charming as Dana. Tell me about her."

"Later. What happened to Gina?"

Beth explained, for what seemed the hundredth time, then added, "She had a perfume bottle on her dresser."

"Gina never wore perfume. Hated being around the stuff."

"I think it held GHB. She was familiar with the drug. Maybe she used it, even gave it to Wade."

"But you don't think she did. Are you being realistic? We all want our friends to be flawless."

Their conversation stalled as Trista scanned the lagoon. "You know, however twisted his reasons, I'm grateful Wade encouraged Dana to come here. She's finding his death a real blow."

"That's understandable."

"I think that if he hadn't died, I wouldn't have let her come near me."

If he hadn't died? Beth banished her traitorous thought.

Trista, shifted against the hard plastic of the chair. "You look like a cornered cat. What's going on?"

Beth squirmed under her scrutiny. "Two people are dead and I'm supposed to believe someone is framing me."

"Framing you?"

Beth closed her eyes and inhaled the warm, moist air as she repeated Evan's concerns and Carl's speculations.

"Carl's full of bull. I'd be a more likely suspect. After Wade tried using Dana against me, I considered hunting him down and hurting him."

"But you were with Harvey and the drug wasn't ordered on your account. Had you ever even heard of the stuff?"

"One of my girls was given Rohypnol during a school function. It took months to piece together her flashbacks. At another party, a couple of guys arrived with a batch of that GHB stuff. Seven of our girls were adversely affected. One is still undergoing addiction therapy. As part of their revised security precautions the school cancelled all dances."

"What happened to the boys?"

"Probation, expulsion. If punishments were more severe, maybe guys would think before acting like jerks."

"What do your students learn about computers?" Beth asked.

"The basics. A bit of programming, the major software packages and the Web. We get some naturals, actually more than you would think, considering we're an all-girl school. Public bias still labels women as non-scientific and computer phobic."

"Here comes Dana," Beth said, as she spotted the girl's long-legged gait. Dana strode toward them, her dark hair plastered against her skull and her brown eyes twinkling with delight.

Beth looked at Trista and saw fulfillment. Whatever fears she had about Dana, she was now a doting parent. Because Wade was dead.

Harvey arrived while Dana was gracefully folding herself into a half lotus. He looked surprisingly fit for a man approaching forty.

He dropped his gym bag onto Trista's lounge and pulled her to her feet and then to the water's edge. Why would Trista let herself be swept away, even by Harvey? Wade's actions had caused her years of pain and had led to a life of isolation, so how could she trust Harvey enough to fall for him in a matter of hours?

Beth watched them splash and tumble through the water. Their casual enjoyment of each other reminded her of her parents, and of how she and Mike had played in the ocean off Mexico.

Harvey and Trista fit each other so well their relationship could be months, not days, old. Maybe they had renewed their friendship through the Internet? For all she knew they had met many times. Maybe Trista had confided Dana's pursuit and Wade's threats months ago?

Harvey had been the first person to examine Wade's body, the one who had started the police thinking about drugs. Why? Would the cause of death be so obvious that a patsy had to be designated?

Who better than Wade's old girlfriend?

Harvey tugged Trista farther from shore until the pounding man-made surf submerged them.

They were each other's alibi.

"They look cute together," Dana said.

Beth shifted her attention to the girl.

"Like old friends." Or old lovers?

"So you guys knew each other forever," Dana said.

"Very nearly. We started kindergarten together."

"Was my dad smart?" Dana asked, shifting into an impossibly twisted full lotus.

Beth thought back over a gap of twenty years. "He preferred having a reputation as a jock. He never studied and he skipped half of his classes, but still graduated with decent marks, so he must have been intelligent."

"He thought university was unnecessary."

"For him it might have been."

Dana looked toward Trista. "Tell me more about the accident and the girl who died." Her voice sounded thick with emotion.

"What did he tell you?"

"That the other driver ran a light; I didn't know Wade was drunk."

"Wade didn't always see the same truth as everyone else."

"We arranged to meet at a Mall entrance on Saturday afternoon. Then we were going to surprise Trista. I thought my dreams of finding my real family had come true."

Had he really wanted to reconcile Trista and Dana, or was he escalating his search for a payoff? She clicked her nails on the arm of her chair. "What time Saturday?"

"Two-forty-five. He even told me which entrance he'd be at. I knew I'd freak if someone from my past just popped up without warning. So I called her. I guess I was hoping she would actually agree to meet me."

"I heard her say no."

"There was still Wade." Dana's eyes pleaded for understanding. "I was late, but I waited at Entrance 51 for a long time expecting him to come for me. When he didn't, I went looking. I had to see him, even if Trista was upset."

"So she knew Wade would be here?" Beth asked.

"I don't know. I said I wanted to meet her. I didn't tell her I would be here, or that Wade would be either."

"He didn't say why it was important to meet you here?"

Dana's hair radiated sunshine as she shook her head. "He said forgiveness was easier to obtain than permission and wired me money for the bus. Trista seems nice. I mean, after she unfroze and we started talking."

"She always was the sympathetic one in our group."

Dana twisted the tooled silver ring that covered half of her index finger. She looked up at Beth, her eyes squinting against the bright sunlight. "That was why he had a chance to hurt her. If you'd resolved your issues with him, Trista wouldn't have been hurt and I'd never have been born."

"Is that what Trista said?" Beth asked.

"She didn't bitch about you, if that's what you think."

Beth reached out for Dana's shoulder. Dana pulled away. Beth rested her hand on the arm of the chair. "I'm certain your adoptive parents, and Trista, are glad you were born."

Dana's voice fell to a whisper. "If I hadn't contacted Wade, maybe he would still be alive."

A chilly certainty ran through Beth. Dana believed Trista had killed Wade.

Spreading her fingers wide to grip the chair arms, Beth asked, "Do you think . . . ?"

Dana gained her footing with minimal effort and maximum grace. She stood with her feet apart and her fists clenched, ready to strike down any slurs on her mother's character. "I don't think anything," she said as she turned and fled.

Dana glanced briefly at Harvey and Trista, then with her shoulders rigid, strode toward the waterslides.

CHAPTER THIRTY-SEVEN

Before lunch, Pete called for a minute of silence and made a brief speech about the passing of two of their own. Then he turned everyone loose on the crisp, cold salads and the spicy fried chicken. The buns were fresh and the berries, topped with real cream, delectable. A few people arrived, indulged, commiserated, then bade farewell until the next reunion. Most remained to relax and enjoy a rare day in the sun.

Beth had long since abandoned her lounge chair and felt she had shaken more hands and kissed more cheeks than a politician seeking office. Everyone promised to keep in touch and exchanged addresses. She asked people how they had enjoyed their stay and what they had done, hoping to piece together who had been where and when they'd been there.

She knew Evan had asked the same questions. She also knew he wouldn't be pleased with her interference.

She scanned the crowd. Joe Small came into view trailing his petite wife and three scrappy kids draped in towels and wet from the wave pool. When she finally separated him from his whiny quartet of followers, he admitted he had been with Wade at the bar. Wade had left with the rest of them, though while some had gone to Pete's room to continue the party, Wade had disappeared saying he was meeting someone.

"I thought he meant you. He told us he was back in

Canada for good. That he was sick of the tropics. Apparently, snorkelling loses its appeal in a way skiing never can."

Pete Hargrove stepped between them.

"Pete," Joe said, "did you see Wade after he left the bar?"

"I saw Carmen McKay in the hotel lobby, making a beeline for him."

Beth felt her stomach lurch and wished she'd forgone the second piece of chicken. "Wade was meeting her?"

Pete winked.

"I thought he was safely settled for the night. I was surprised he ended up in your room."

"Was he drunk?"

"Well, I haven't seen him drink in nearly twenty years so it's hard to say what his capacity is, but yeah, I'd say he was close to the limit."

"Had he been drinking heavily?"

"Not as much as Joey, here, but then no one does."

"Where did you go last night?"

"Whoa. I don't know what you're getting at, but Gina wasn't my style," Pete said.

"Then you won't mind answering."

Pete and Joe exchanged glances, then Pete said, "After the dancing died out, we sent the wives upstairs and a bunch of us caught a cab downtown to see some strippers. Then we hit an after hours club. Satisfied, Nancy Drew?"

Joe nudged him in the ribs and tilted his head, indicating they should join their buddies and families.

Janice Tyler and her companion strolled into the grotto wearing matching swimsuits. Beth joined them at the buffet. She plucked a square of cheesecake from the disappearing array, then added a cluster of grapes and a couple of cheese cubes.

In response to her question about their whereabouts on Friday night, Janice eagerly told her of their experience in the casino. They returned to their room just before three. Janice swore she had seen Carmen still hanging around the lobby, alone and looking lonesome.

So much for the theory that she had left with Wade.

"I tried to interest her in a drink in our room. She was rude about refusing."

"What about last night, after you left the dance?"

"Straight to bed. Can't do two late nights in a row anymore." After they finished filling their plates, they sauntered toward the bank of deckchairs.

Bobbie Dillan showed up late and alone. Beth waved and Bobbie veered toward her. "Aaron refused to come with me. He's uncomfortable about the stares and comments. I'll admit this reunion has been a real acid test."

"You did surprise everyone."

The silence stretched while Bobbie loaded a plate with fried chicken. Beth asked how she and Aaron had spent Friday evening.

Bobbie looked sheepish at first, then smiled wide enough to show off her newly straightened and brilliantly white teeth. "We rented the African theme room. It's the first time I've had a chance to act out the role of damsel in distress."

Bobbie's bottom lip jutted forward into a beautiful pout. "All through high school I fantasized about dressing up in a cheerleader outfit. I hated being a quarterback."

"Why were you on the football team?" Beth asked.

Her shoulders rose and her pout turned into a scowl. "My father insisted. He used to beat me for wearing my sister's clothes. Said I was a pervert. Wanted me to prove I was all-male.

"Dad finally got the whole picture, painted in primary colours, when my sister asked me to be an usher at her wedding. I arrived wearing a gorgeous green dress that rivalled the bridesmaids' gowns. He hasn't spoken to me since." She shrugged again. "Everything has a price."

"Does the rest of your family accept your choice?"

"I've left most of my first life behind. I'd appreciate your not mentioning my past if we should meet on the street."

Beth promised silence, then asked, "Did anyone ever threaten to tell your employers about your past life?"

Bobbie stiffened, "Why are you asking?"

"Just a thought. This group has a few people with secrets they would like to keep."

She felt a prickle up her spine and turned to see Carl Lauder leering at them. When Bobbie rushed away to greet other guests, Carl darted to Beth's side. "So you're getting cozy with the freaks now are you? You certainly have weird taste in friends."

"You used to be buddies."

"It used to be a he."

Beth scowled at him.

"What are you asking everyone?" he demanded.

"Can't I talk to old friends?"

"You're doing more than talking. I know grilling when I see it. You're just kicking up dirt. Go along with the accident theory your cop buddy is spouting. You're engaged to his partner, so they'll make the system work in mysterious ways."

Beth wanted to slap his smirk away, but instead hid her nausea. "I'm asking people if they saw Wade after he left the bar. The police have already asked the same thing."

"Are you sure? Maybe they don't want to prove you met him."

"Gina saw him after I left the hotel."

"Or, she lied for you. It wouldn't be the first time a friend did that. Now that she's dead, she can't change her story."

"Carl, you're a louse," Bobbie said as she approached them. "You always did enjoy picking on women. That's why they kicked you off the force, right? I heard all about that incident on the streets of Vancouver, and I do mean everything, so why don't you stop hassling Beth and maybe I won't tell everyone here the details."

Carl flushed, then blanched. He blustered for a

moment, then turned, and rushed toward the exit.

"You scared him."

"Just reminded him that his past could land him in jail. Believe me, the less you know about it, the cleaner you'll feel."

"I could have handled him."

"Of course you could, but us girls have to stick together. He always was afraid of anyone bigger than him, and mean to the rest of the world."

Beth's gaze travelled Bobbie's entire six-foot length. Her arms and shoulders were well muscled and capable of physically subduing the out-of-shape Carl. And her wrists were covered in bracelets and her nails glowed red.

Beth spotted Ms. McKay walking in the direction of the exit. Turning her attention back to Bobbie, she said, "Look, thanks for your help, but I'm going to catch Carmen McKay before she escapes."

"Ms. McKay," Beth said. "I haven't had a chance to speak to you."

Ms. McKay's pixie face brightened into a smile as she tilted her head to one side. "You must forgive me, but I've met so many students this past couple of days, that it's difficult to put a name to a face."

Beth introduced herself, knowing she had been the centre of too much gossip for Carmen to be unaware of her identity.

"I understand you met Wade in the hotel lobby late Friday night."

"I was returning from a visit with some dear

friends. It's so good to return to Edmonton and see people I've taught with over the years."

"I didn't realize you'd left town."

"A silly misunderstanding a couple of years back. I chose to move to another school district rather than have my name slandered fighting the allegations of adolescent boys. They have such active and lurid imaginations."

Beth swallowed a nasty rejoinder. "Where was Wade going when he left you?"

"Well, he said he was meeting a lady. That wouldn't have been you would it?"

"Definitely not. He didn't mention any names or tell you where or why they were meeting?"

She sighed dramatically. "Well, I told him my escort had been called away on an emergency, leaving me at loose ends. He was solicitous and promised we could get together on Saturday afternoon, but he did not elaborate on his evening's activities."

Ms. McKay rose on her toes and waved her fingers. "Look, Arnie is standing over there all alone. You know I haven't greeted him properly and it's nearly time to say goodbye. Do you know if he's married?"

Beth closed her eyes and shook her head. She refused to be part of this woman's avaricious hunt.

"Oh, well, I don't see the little woman hanging on his arm, so even if he is, she must not be with him." Without another word she turned and swaying in time to the Calypso music, danced away.

Beth looked around the thinning crowd, hoping to

spot someone who might have been around late Friday night. Suzanne and her companions stood near the punch bowl. Suzanne's bikini seemed borderline illegal. Rhonda had opted for a tent-like cover up. Katy wore a thigh-length blouse over her one-piece suit. They all wore sunglasses. She wove through the clusters of people until she stood behind them.

"Did you enjoy your stay, ladies?"

"Beth, it was one of the best yet. You must plan the next one for a convention centre, too. We met the nicest people," Suzanne gushed.

"Did you see Wade Friday night, while you were out with your new friends?"

"Sorry," Suzanne focused an intimidating stare on her friends. "We can't help you, can we ladies?"

Maggie Hartwell ambushed Beth as she watched Suzanne lead her friends toward the row of private cabanas. "It's been just the best reunion Beth. I do hope you plan all the future ones. It's been so wonderful seeing you again."

Beth wished she could remember more about the woman, but the details refused to come. In answer to her question about where she was late Friday night, Maggie just laughed and said she hadn't seen 2:30 AM since she breast-fed little Jessie almost fifteen years earlier.

CHAPTER THIRTY-EIGHT

Mike walked into his father's hospital room hoping the Sunday morning sunshine and clear prairie sky foretold a good day. His mother greeted him with a tearful smile, overjoyed because his father's speech was clearer and he had moved his hand a few inches farther than he had managed the day before. Mike felt ten pounds of fear float away; he moved his neck to loosen the tension that had stiffened his shoulders into solid oak beams. Perhaps he could return to Edmonton soon.

First, he had to attend that orientation session on Monday. Of course, it was more important that his mother and brother attend, because they would be the ones dealing with his father's recovery on a daily basis.

He had almost lost his father once, and vowed to do whatever it took to make up for his neglect. He would take a leave and return to help his mother. And until his dad was back to normal, or as close to it as he was going to get, he would visit often.

Beth would understand his neglect. She always understood and forgave the pressures that kept them separated. It was one of the most annoying things about her.

His father groaned in his sleep and Mike jumped back to the present. After a single twitch of his head, his dad settled back into his eerie stillness.

Mike had wasted too much time waiting for Beth to set a date. No one knew how much time they had left, maybe years, but maybe only hours. Not committing to each other fully was no longer enough. Somehow, he had to convince her to marry him, soon.

Mike felt his mother's hand grip his arm. "He's got a long stay in bed before he gets out of here," she said. "You don't have to hang around. I know you're needed in Edmonton."

"There's nothing more important happening there than what's going on here."

"Isn't Beth in trouble?"

"Evan will look after her."

"His wife is having problems with her pregnancy. He should be spending time with her."

"Don't you want me here?"

"Of course, I do, but there is little you can do for your father right now."

"I should stay for that orientation."

"There will be others." She smiled as she patted his arm. "Just return when you can."

Mothers always seemed to know how to make you feel guiltier than you already did. Still, Mike saw the logic of her words.

He left the hospital room with the excuse of getting coffee and toast. Once in the lounge he phoned Evan, hoping the case had resolved itself and he wouldn't feel this pressing need to return.

Evan sounded tired and his first words justified his fatigue. "It's a girl, Mike. Debra delivered in a couple of hours. They are both healthy, but I'm beat."

"You'll be taking time off now. Are you finished at West Ed Mall?"

"We've had a second death."

"Who?" he asked, kicking himself for being out of touch.

"Beth's friend Gina. Someone hit her over the head and tossed her into the Jacuzzi."

"She phoned Beth last night."

"So I heard," Evan said, then proceeded to relate their other findings.

"Who was that Wade guy, anyway?"

"I've put out feelers. Seems he's been out of Canada since signing onto a cruise ship right after high school. Moved around a lot, different jobs, different islands. No wife or girlfriend on even a semi-permanent basis, no close friends."

"What else?"

"He worked in resorts and crossed paths with the dead woman recently. I've got calls into every place he's worked over the past five years. Half of Edmonton heads south in January, so he could have met other old friends too. We'll crosscheck his places of employment with the travel records of reunion participants."

"Anything that points to a motive?"

"Maybe we're dealing with drug trafficking."

"Is the woman's death linked to him?"

"Different method, but we found some of the drug that killed him in her room."

"My dad's improving and Mom is tired of my face,

so I'm returning to Edmonton this afternoon. Just hold off passing the case to someone else. Please."

"Don't worry, it's Sunday here too. I'll hold on to it until tomorrow when Debra is ready for discharge."

CHAPTER THIRTY-NINE

By the time Beth returned to her lounge chair to analyze the information she had gathered, the crowd filling the Waterpark had multiplied. The reunion group remained clustered in their corner. The conversations Beth heard ranged from laughing reminiscences to whispered confidences.

She closed her eyes and let relaxation seep into her. The reunion was a success and her part in it seemed worth the effort she had expended. She felt a hand on her arm and opened one eye.

Evan stood beside her, his demeanour sober.

"More bad news?"

"You were on Grand Cayman a year ago February."

"Great place, but pricey." Beth wondered where his question fit into the events of the past few days.

"Did you meet Wade Hamelin while you were there?"

"No."

"Never ran into him on the beach?"

"I thought he worked on Bali."

"He worked on Grand Cayman then, at the resort where you stayed."

"I swear I hadn't seen Wade from the time he left Edmonton twenty years ago, until this past Friday."

"He was asked to resign from a couple of places

because of his conduct with guests. He considered himself a lady's man and sometimes pushed too hard."

Beth recalled Trista's nightmarish tale and wondered how hard Wade had pushed the hotel guests. She knew that women were sometimes assaulted in resorts. Some employees gambled the victim wouldn't want to hang around pressing charges and testifying against them.

She thought back to that Caribbean vacation. She had flown in, spent two nights on Grand Cayman, then a week sailing, and finally another two nights on the Island before flying home.

"It didn't happen. That resort is a big place. I never saw him."

"It's tough to prove a negative." Evan looked sheepish. "I'm taking leave to help Debra with the baby, so I'll pass this case to someone else tomorrow."

He touched her wrist and looked into her eyes. "We're doing what we can to find out what happened."

"But it looks more and more like I was involved, doesn't it?"

"I wish I could stay on the case, but . . ." He shrugged.

"Family always comes first."

"No one admits to seeing Wade after Gina saw him at the door of your room."

"You know I wasn't there."

"Your friend Harvey is your staunchest advocate, but you have a lot of friends here."

Beth turned to look where Evan was staring. Her classmates were watching them.

"They wouldn't lie for me."

"Gina might have."

"She told you she saw him at my door."

"That would be hard to cover up since his body was found in the bed, but if the timing was different, say she saw him half an hour earlier, or maybe she did recognize you."

"You think I killed her to keep her from talking? If that was true, why would I tell you she'd phoned me?"

"Why didn't she call your cell?"

She turned toward her friends. "I forgot to turn it on after the speeches. Now, unless you're prepared to arrest me, I have duties. Give my best to Debra."

Beth felt him retreat. For the moment he was her enemy. At least he had given her a bit of information that wouldn't work against her. Wade must have been searching for a job in Canada not to rediscover the joys of snow, but to escape a bad reputation.

Beth turned and watched the ant-like kids on the waterslides. Some guy was gliding through the sky with only a bungee cord to prevent him from smashing into the bottom of a pool.

Perhaps Wade needed money. Maybe he had tried extortion on someone other than Trista. Someone with more to lose and less conscience.

She scanned the crowd, searching for a glimmer of animosity, a triumphant smile, a satisfied grin, but saw only sympathy and pity. Harvey sent her an encouraging smile, then strode over to where she stood. "His news wasn't good?"

"He's taking time to be with his new daughter."

"That's the good news, what was the bad?"

"Before signing on to help with this damn reunion, I hadn't heard from most of these people in two decades. Why would one of them hate me enough to frame me for murder?"

"They think Wade was killed? Last night you said it was accidental."

"He was murdered and Gina was killed because she figured out who he was with. That same person wants Evan to think I killed them both."

"You had no reason to kill Wade and of course you couldn't kill Gina. They have to look elsewhere."

"I stayed on an island where Wade was working. Add that to the fact that someone used my computer and charge account to order the drug that killed him and tell me what you think."

"Either you've become very careless or someone stole your identity."

"That's just what I told him."

"Maybe they didn't intend to harm you?"

"How does that work?"

"They didn't want records pointing at them and you were an easy target."

"Then why phone the police and tell them where to look for evidence?"

"That does indicate malice."

"Wade hurt someone enough that they wanted him dead. I'll scrutinize every day of the past twenty years if I have to, but I'll find out who that person is. Evan was doing that when he discovered I'd vacationed on that island. He might keep looking. Mike would, but do you think some other detective will be that meticulous?"

"We will figure out what's going on."

Beth took a calming breath, then another. Getting hysterical wasn't going to help solve anything.

Her classmates had secrets, and if Wade had learned what they were, he could have been blackmailing several people. Trista had Dana to hide. Bobbie had her new life to protect. Even Suzanne and her group wanted to avoid scandal.

Harvey took Beth's arm. "Come on."

Beth let him lead her toward her classmates. She would have to face them eventually, and it might as well be sooner.

A slender, young girl stood next to Jasmine, a young man held her hand. Beth recognized Jasmine's daughter Tiffany and her boyfriend Todd. Tiffany's honey blonde hair was the shade Beth remembered, but the green streak running through it did little to enhance her beauty. Beth grimaced; she must be getting old if she was criticizing kids' hair fashions.

Trista and Dana joined the group. Like Dana, Tiffany wore a skimpy bikini and floppy sandals. It was surprising how much girls of that age resembled each other with their slender bodies, their unmarked faces, and their predilection to tattoos and the piercing of body parts. Dana had a rose tattooed on her shoulder; Tiffany wore a snake curling up her leg. Tiffany had more earrings fastened to one ear than Dana wore on both. Their hairstyles were different too. Tiffany's looked as if she had just been roused from bed. Dana's hugged and emphasized the shape of her skull.

Dana seemed older, perhaps because the uncertainty surrounding her birth and the quest for her parents had marred her short life. Beth studied their mothers and wondered why the girls looked like sisters. Her gaze met Jasmine's and she saw panic in her friend's eyes.

"Tiffany," Beth said as she approached the group, "I thought you couldn't make it this weekend."

Tiffany held tight to her mother's hand. "I heard the news and figured Mom would be pretty upset, so I decided that even if she had told Hollis and me to stay away, I'd better come."

Beth kept her gaze locked on Jasmine as she asked, "Why didn't your mother want you here?"

"She thought I'd be bored, though how I could be bored in this mall, I don't know."

"And Hollis?"

"I told you he had a previous commitment," Jasmine said, pushing Tiffany aside.

"Tiffany, why don't you and Todd show Dana the best waterslide? Your mother and I have to talk."

Tiffany frowned. "I don't think I should."

"Go with them," Jasmine said.

Tiffany looked at her mother, obviously puzzled, then toward Dana, who smiled. The girls linked arms with Todd and hurried toward the maze of waterslides.

Beth pulled Jasmine toward the rear of the secluded grove. Trista and Harvey followed.

"She's Wade's daughter, isn't she," Beth demanded.

Jasmine stared at the cement floor, shaking her head.

"I never saw it before, but then why should I," Beth continued. "When did it happen? It must have been that same summer. It was, wasn't it?" Beth tightened her grip on Jasmine's shoulder.

Jasmine stepped backward, her expression belligerent. "Yes, he was her father, though he didn't know it and neither does she."

Beth tried to clear her thoughts. The idea was . . . it didn't make sense. "But he killed Sharon."

"Yes, he did. But his punishment was a joke. I thought I could do better. I sat in my car and watched his house every night and finally one night he got into his dad's car and drove to the river. At first, I was just going to call the police and report him for driving while suspended, but when he parked and started into the woods carrying a bottle of booze my plan changed. My dad kept his hunting rifle in the trunk. I decided I could shoot him and throw his body in the river and no one would know. He was always telling people he was going to leave town and never return.

"But it was a trick and before I could find him, he came at me from behind and grabbed the gun. He raped me and left me in the middle of nowhere."

"Then you discovered you were pregnant and married Ralph?"

"Ralph knew she wasn't his, but said he didn't care who the father was. The minute he saw her he knew—she looked like Wade from day one. No one ever thought about the resemblance, maybe because Wade had left town the day after he hurt me."

"Why kill him now?"

"I didn't do that, Beth. I would have back then, but now I have Tiffany."

Jasmine straightened her shoulders and lifted her chin. "And I'm getting married again, to someone I can love forever. I'd never risk hurting them even if it meant avenging Sharon. Besides, I never even saw Wade this weekend."

"That's not true." The words came from the fringe of the group that had gathered to witness their confrontation.

Beth turned as Katy stepped in front of Harvey. Her hands were folded as if pleading for forgiveness.

"We saw you with him."

"If that's true, why didn't you tell the police?"

"They might have asked who I was with when I saw you."

"And he was someone you'd picked up? That's no revelation."

"Suzanne said the media would make our behaviour a public spectacle and my family would learn about our weekends. I couldn't hurt them like that; I couldn't risk losing everything. But I can't let your lie hurt Beth. Rhonda, you'll back me up, won't you?"

Rhonda glanced at Suzanne and then lowered her

gaze to her clasped hands. After a long time she nodded. She looked at Suzanne and mouthed the word "sorry."

Jasmine raised her hands and shrugged her shoulders. "Okay, so I saw him, but I walked by without a backward glance. What happened to him after that, I don't know."

"You lied about being in your room when I knocked. Did you lie about taking a sleeping pill? Was it GHB?"

"No, it's doctor prescribed and I can prove it. I just went to get a book from my car. Leaving the hotel isn't a crime."

Beth watched Evan approach the group and stand on the fringe. She acknowledged him with a glance, then turned her attention back to Jasmine.

"You didn't tell the police that you'd left your room or that you'd seen Wade."

"The last thing I need is to get caught up in some murder investigation. Hollis is wealthy, he's in politics and definitely not in a position to have his life touched by scandal."

"You knew Wade would be here though, didn't you? That's why you kept Tiffany and Hollis away. That's why you were so calm when you supposedly found out. He saw that picture of us in Mexico and figured out that Tiffany was his child. He was blackmailing you."

Jasmine's bottom lip trembled. Tears welled in her eyes. "He knew about Tiffany and about my engagement to Hollis. He wanted me to finance his new life. I was going to. But on the drive here, I realized his demands would never end and that eventually I had to tell Tiffany the truth. When I saw him Friday night, I told him to do his worst. I figured if Hollis couldn't understand he wasn't the man I wanted to marry."

"Or maybe you slipped him that GHB?"

"No, I swear," Jasmine's voice rose, then faded into a whisper. "Ask Dawn. I saw her pull into the parking lot while I was with Wade. I left so she wouldn't see me, but she must have seen him."

Dawn took a sip of water. "You're mistaken. I was home with my husband."

Suzanne spoke in a voice that carried throughout the quiet crowd. "He died of a GHB overdose? No one said that before. Dawn lost her kid because she was addicted to the stuff. Lionel threatened to leave her if she started using again."

Dawn searched the faces surrounding her, then straightened her shoulders, her chin rose in defiance.

"She's lying. We're perfectly happy. She'll say anything to steal him away from me."

"What about your son?" Suzanne asked.

"My lawyer is confident I'll get Brendan back. It will just take time."

"Dawn, what's in that water bottle you're always carrying around?" Beth asked.

Dawn slipped the bottle into her tote bag. "Water, what else would it be? It's important to stay hydrated when you're working out or dieting."

"Are you willing to have it tested?"

Her panicked expression gave Beth the answer.

"Did Wade find out you were using? Did he threaten to tell? You would have lost your son and your husband."

Dawn pulled the bottle from her bag and held it up, her charm bracelet glittered in the sunlight. "I told you it's just water. See, absolutely clear spring water."

Beth reached out, Dawn pulled her hand back.

"That's what Gina wanted to tell me, what she thought was so funny. It was your charm bracelet she saw, wasn't it?"

"Now you're being really silly. We didn't have a history. We barely even spoke to each other."

"Why were you at the hotel so late?"

"I forgot something. Came back to retrieve it."

"You kept in touch with Wade," Evan interrupted. "We've accessed his e-mail account. Seems these two had deep, heartfelt conversations about their old classmates. She passed him a lot of gossip."

"Liar," Dawn screamed. "You're all out to get me. You always were and you were the worst." She pointed at Beth. "You have everything. You never had to worry about a date, or money for university. If I'd had your life I could be successful too."

"You won the lottery."

"And Lionel married me to get my money, but I wouldn't let him touch one penny of it until I got my son back. Wade sympathized when I told him Lionel was cheating on me with the likes of you," she said, glaring at Suzanne.

"He phoned me, said Lionel was here with you. I came back to find him."

"Lionel is my friend and trainer. Nothing more," Suzanne said.

Dawn looked around at the crowd. As the pause stretched, her scowl relaxed into a slight frown, tears welled in her eyes.

"Wade grabbed my water bottle. He said unless I paid him to keep quiet, he'd turn it over to my ex's lawyer. Fingerprints, saliva and all then I'd never get near Brendan again."

"So you took him to my room and killed him," Beth demanded.

"I suggested we go somewhere private to negotiate because I didn't have any money left to give him. Wade said your room was empty, but it deserved to see some action. He wasn't interested in me though. He was too busy pawing through your clothes. I doctored his drink. Figured that would knock him out.

"But you can't blame me for his death. It was an accident. He was supposed to wake up after the committee arrived for our morning meeting. It was a joke. I even gift wrapped him. You would have looked like the cheating whore you are," she said, looking directly at Beth.

"But Wade would still have been a threat."

"Not if the evidence was gone."

"You knew mixing that drug with alcohol was deadly," Beth said.

"Prove it."

"Gina saw you go into Beth's room. You were afraid she'd eventually identify you, and you killed her," Beth said.

Dawn looked toward Evan, her lips twitched with a tiny smile. "Prove it."

"Fingerprints on the murder weapon match yours," Evan said.

"I wiped, . . ." Dawn stopped speaking, but her expression darkened when she realized what she had revealed. "You lied."

Evan nodded.

Dawn clutched her tote bag to her chest. She looked at Suzanne. "Well counsellor. Do you advise me to remain silent?"

Suzanne stared at her, but said nothing.

"What the hell. I've already lost Brendan and now Lionel. What more can you take away from me? My freedom? What's that worth?

"Gina was toying with me. I knew when she was ready, she would identify me. I waited in her closet, figured I would drug her, throw her in the Jacuzzi and watch her drown. But she called Beth, said she'd remembered. That moved up my timeline. I hit her. I threw her in the water, hoping you'd believe she'd slipped."

CHAPTER FORTY

Beth wandered around her dimly lit room as she dressed for the dinner theatre. She was going to attend because it was her final obligation.

She was finally alone, though it had taken hours to convince her friends that she would survive.

Soon after they left, Evan had phoned to say Dawn had signed a written confession, against the advice of her legal aid lawyer. Apparently she had started using the drug to aid weight loss, then to relax, and finally to entice Lionel. She had used Beth's name when ordering the drug, so nothing could be traced back to her.

Gentle knocking broke into Beth's thoughts. Would they never leave her alone? Who had they sent to collect her this time?

She grabbed her purse and opened the door.

Mike stepped into the room, arms crossed, and a smile turning up the corners of his lips. "I hear you resolved that little matter without any help from me. Should I feel unnecessary?"

She felt her anger melt and her heart fill. "I had lots of help. I'm glad to see you."

She hated having to say the words, hated hurting him, but he had to know she was jinxed. "Mike, I've learned some things about myself this weekend, and I don't think it's fair to keep on with our relationship."

He pulled her close and rested his chin on her head.

"I agree, we should change a few things. I think you should meet my family. Let's plan to drive to Saskatchewan as a married couple. I've arranged to use the Marketplace Chapel here in the mall and we have the licence from last summer. I've invited your friends and hauled Evan along to be best man. All you have to do is pick out a bridesmaid or two."

Beth looked up into Mike's face, studying his character lines.

Was this what she wanted? No planning, no fuss, just lots of people who had proved themselves to be true friends and a man who wanted to remain at her side forever.

"You're not going to change, are you? Demand that I quit work and raise lots of kids? Or want to move back to Saskatchewan and live on a farm?"

"What you see is what you get."

"You wanted a big wedding," she hedged.

"No, I just wanted a wedding."

"Your family won't mind?"

"They're busy right now, but they will be delighted to know we've stopped procrastinating."

"My parents. I have to call them."

"They're waiting in the chapel. By the way, you neglected to tell them what's been going on."

"I didn't want to worry them."

"You're supposed to share troubles with family. Let's get out of here so the bellboy can take your stuff to the honeymoon suite. That Lorelei is as good at arranging difficult details as you claimed."

Beth looked at Mike, then at the truck bed. Maybe they'd try it out on their first anniversary.

D. M. WYMAN was born and raised in Edmonton, Alberta. She spent her working years typing, cataloguing, and selling books while raising two sons. Eventually she took a year off to devote herself to fulfilling her dream of writing and publishing a novel. One year later and novel in hand she decided to continue volunteering, travelling, and writing full-time. Most recently in Greece, she has travelled extensively throughout Europe, and across Canada. D. M. Wyman's first novel, *Reunions Are Deadly,* is set in her hometown of Edmonton where she lives with her husband and two cats.